"I've missed you..." smiling down in... "Did you miss m...

More than anything observing the way he was with Bekka. *And more than you'll ever know.*

With more than a little effort, she blocked and shut down her feelings. She was *not* about to own up to what she was thinking or say the words out loud.

That was all she needed to do, Claire upbraided herself. If Levi had a clue as to what she was thinking, he would just take it to mean that he could move back into their apartment and, just like that, it would be business as usual.

Would that be so bad? she questioned herself.

Yes! Yes, it would be that bad. She'd be back to spending all her time taking care of the baby and missing Levi, while he'd be spending all his free time away from her.

Supposedly securing their future...if she were to believe him.

She had to remember how that felt—missing him, being taken for granted—she silently counseled herself.

But all that staying angry required effort. Effort that was hard to maintain when part of her kept longing for the touch of his hand, the feel of his lips on hers.

* * *

MONTANA MAVERICKS:
WHAT HAPPENED AT THE WEDDING?
A weekend Rust Creek Falls will never forget!

Dear Reader,

I have always loved Westerns, something that I shared with my very Polish father. We watched TV together at night when I was a little girl. I watched every single episodic Western TV show he saw fit to throw at me. I even memorized all the theme songs. (I am available for weddings and kids' parties.) I not only watched Westerns, I *lived* Westerns, adding myself into each and every story. (I was the hero's girlfriend or wisecracking sister in every episode. Bet you didn't know the Lone Ranger had a sister, did you?)

With this kind of background, you can see why I jumped at the chance to write another Montana Mavericks book.

In this story, for once the couple is married when the book begins, but there are strong signs that they might not be that way by the end of it. It's the usual story: a couple, madly in love, gets married...and then gets caught up in the details of maintaining the marriage. He's away all day, working. She's home with a cranky baby. Claire Strickland feels neglected, and Levi Wyatt feels exhausted and misunderstood. When she runs off with the baby to her grandparents' boarding house, Levi knows he has to go after her and straighten things out or their fledgling marriage will be over before it really ever started.

As ever, dearest reader, I would like to thank you for taking the time to read my latest effort to entertain you. And from the bottom of my heart, I wish you someone to love who loves you back.

Marie Ferrarella

Do You Take This Maverick?

Marie Ferrarella

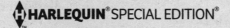

HARLEQUIN® SPECIAL EDITION®

Special thanks and acknowledgment to Marie Ferrarella for her contribution to the Montana Mavericks: What Happened at the Wedding? continuity.

ISBN-13: 978-0-373-65901-2

Do You Take This Maverick?

Recycling programs for this product may not exist in your area.

Printed in U.S.A.

USA TODAY bestselling and RITA® Award-winning author **Marie Ferrarella** has written more than two hundred books for Harlequin, some under the name Marie Nicole. Her romances are beloved by fans worldwide. Visit her website, marieferrarella.com.

Books by Marie Ferrarella

Harlequin Special Edition

Matchmaking Mamas

Diamond in the Ruff
Dating for Two
Wish Upon a Matchmaker
Ten Years Later...
A Perfectly Imperfect Match
Once Upon a Matchmaker

The Fortunes of Texas: Cowboy Country

Mendoza's Secret Fortune

The Fortunes of Texas:
Welcome to Horseback Hollow

Lassoed by Fortune

Harlequin Romantic Suspense

Mission: Cavanaugh Baby
Cavanaugh on Duty
A Widow's Guilty Secret
Cavanaugh's Surrender
Cavanaugh Rules
Cavanaugh's Bodyguard

Visit the Author Profile page
at Harlequin.com for more titles.

To
Gail Chasan,
who is always
in my
corner.
Thank you.

Prologue

"I don't see what you're so mad about."

Levi Wyatt stared at his wife of two years in absolute confusion. The second he had opened the door and walked into their room, Claire had lit into him, reading him the riot act.

Granted, it was almost dawn and he had never stayed out anywhere *near* this late before, but that was no reason for Claire to be so upset.

This was definitely a side of his wife he had never seen before.

Industrious, ambitious and hardworking, Levi rarely, if ever, took any time off from his job at the furniture store. As the recently promoted store manager, most of the time he even worked on the weekends, but this weekend—the Fourth of July—he'd taken off to escort

Claire to a wedding in Rust Creek Falls. He could have skipped it, personally, but it seemed to be really important to Claire that he attend, too. Her grandparents were putting them up for the weekend at the boarding house that they ran.

The wedding was held in the town's park, and it was a great afternoon. The ceremony was crowded and joyous, the reception even more so. A few of the attendees had decided to get up a little friendly game of poker. Levi wasn't quite sure why, but he was *really* tempted by the game, so he'd joined in.

Since he, Claire and their eight-month-old daughter, Bekka, were all spending the weekend at the boarding house, he felt that Claire wouldn't lack for company while he was gone. Especially since Melba Strickland, Claire's grandma, had graciously offered to babysit so the couple could enjoy the wedding together. This seemed to be the perfect opportunity for him to knock off a little steam.

Besides, he noticed that Claire was busy talking to a woman she knew at the reception when he'd allowed himself to be lured away by the promise of a little harmless diversion.

It was only supposed to be for an hour—two tops.

It had run over.

Way over.

But that still wasn't any reason for Claire to explode this way.

"Oh, you don't, do you?" Claire cried heatedly. Up until this point she had managed to keep her ever-growing discontent under control. She'd never allowed Levi to even catch a glimpse of it, just as she wouldn't dream of letting him see her without her makeup on or with her hair looking anything but perfect. For Claire, it was all about maintaining the illusion of perfection. It always had been.

But tonight, for some reason, she was feeling rather light-headed, although all she'd had to drink at the reception was some of the wedding punch. Despite her petite frame, punch wouldn't affect her like this, she reasoned.

Still, because of her light-headedness, her discontent had slipped out of its usual restraints, and before she knew it, the second Levi had walked into their room at the boarding house, she was giving it to her husband with both barrels.

"No," Levi answered, standing his ground and waiting for Claire to say something that made sense to him, "I don't. I've been working really hard lately, putting in some really long hours. I came to the wedding because *you* wanted to come and when this poker game came up, I didn't see the harm in taking a little time off—"

"Didn't see the harm?" Claire echoed incredulously. Her eyes narrowed into angry, accusing slits. "No, you wouldn't, would you? Well, I'll tell you what the harm is. The harm is that you just walked off and left me— *again*." Not wanting to wake up anyone at the boarding house, she struggled to keep from shouting at him, but it wasn't easy.

"Again? What *again*?" he demanded, stunned. "Claire, what are you talking about? When did I leave you?"

Was he serious? He couldn't possibly be as clueless as he was pretending to be, could he?

"When *didn't* you leave me?" Claire countered, her anger all but running over like a boiling pot of water. "You're always going off out of town to some sales meetings or other. And if it's not a meeting, then it's a *seminar.*" She said the word as if it was a lie that he fed her. "I never get to see you anymore," she complained.

Levi felt his own temper surging, something that almost *never* happened. Ordinarily, he could put up with his wife's fluctuating moods, but right now he felt as if he'd had more than he could stand.

"You're seeing me now." Levi spread his hands wide, as if to highlight his presence. "I'm standing right here," he pointed out.

Was he mocking her? His attitude just kept fueling her anger. "You know what I mean."

"No, I *don't* know what you mean," he told her, feeling more and more bewildered and put upon by the second. "I'm going to those sales meetings and seminars because my job demands it. I'm doing it for you and the baby," Levi stressed.

But Claire saw it differently. "You're doing it to get *away* from me and the baby."

Levi blew out a long breath as he gave up. There was no reasoning with her. "You're tired, you don't know what you're saying," Levi concluded, feeling rather desperate. He just wanted this to stop.

Her big brown eyes—eyes he had fallen in love with

the first time he saw her—were all but shooting daggers at him. "Oh, so now I'm just crazy?"

Where had that come from? "I didn't say that," Levi insisted.

She was twisting everything, he thought helplessly. He felt as if he had stepped into quicksand and was sinking fast, no matter how hard he tried to pull himself free.

"Maybe you didn't *say* it but that's what you implied," Claire retorted haughtily. "And who could blame me if I was crazy—which I'm *not*," Claire underscored. "The only one I get to talk to all day is a colicky, crying baby. Don't get me wrong, Levi, I love Bekka, but you're never around." It was an angry accusation, one she dared him to deny.

"Yes, I am," Levi insisted. "I come home to you every night," Levi told her.

"Sure, you come home," she jeered. "You come home to fall into bed, dead asleep before your head hits the pillow."

"I put in long hours, Claire, and I'm tired," Levi tried to explain.

Claire's back went up as she instantly took offense at what she thought he was implying. "Oh, and I don't and I'm not?"

Levi threw up his hands, thoroughly frustrated. He had stayed longer at the game than he had intended and lost money, to boot. He hadn't meant for any of that to happen. He wasn't really sure *why* it had happened. But he knew that her anger was way out of proportion.

"Look, let's not get into this now," he pleaded. "I'm sorry, okay?"

"No, it's not okay—and you're not sorry," she told him angrily. "But I am. I'm sorry I ever met you. I'm sorry I ever married you!"

Levi was close to being speechless. "Claire, what are you saying?"

Heightened fury was all but etched into her fine features and had colored her cheeks to a bright shade of pink.

"What I'm saying is that it's over," she retorted furiously. "I made a mistake. We *both* made a mistake. We should have never gotten married in the first place."

All this because he stayed out playing poker too long? He couldn't believe what he was hearing. "Claire—"

"Get out!" she cried. Circling him, she put her hands on his back and started pushing him out the door into the hallway. "Get out now!"

"Claire—" It was all Levi could get out of his mouth. He was completely stunned and unable to even understand how they had gotten to this impasse so quickly.

"Now!" she yelled, managing to shove him out all the way only because she had caught him so completely off guard.

The second he was across the threshold and in the hall, Claire pulled off her wedding ring.

"Here, I don't want this anymore, either!" she cried, throwing her wedding ring at him.

The next second she slammed the door shut behind him.

He heard the *click* and knew she'd flipped the lock. Claire had the only key.

Levi stood there in front of the door to their room for several moments, dazed and wondering if he was hallucinating all this for some reason. What had just happened seemed to have come out of nowhere.

This trip was supposed to have picked up Claire's spirits. Instead, he felt that he had just witnessed his marriage falling apart.

What the hell had just happened here? Levi wondered. He hadn't a clue.

As he walked away from the door, Levi heard Bekka beginning to wail from inside the room.

"You and me both, kid," he murmured under his breath. "You and me both."

Chapter One

Almost a month had gone by since the disastrous night of the wedding, and Levi *still* didn't know exactly what had happened. What he did know was that he wanted his wife back.

He missed her.

Missed the baby.

Missed being a married man more than he had ever thought possible.

In one all-too-quick swoop his orderly world had fallen into a state of formless chaos, and he absolutely hated it. He felt directionless. When he and Claire had been together, his life had had purpose, he'd had goals. Now he was just blindly going from one end of the day to the other. He still showed up for work at the furniture store every morning, but he lacked his usual energy, feeling lost and so alone that he literally ached.

Without Claire, absolutely nothing seemed to make any sense to him anymore.

Initially, as he had walked back to his truck right after Claire had thrown him out, his own anger at what he felt was her uncalled-for reaction to his late arrival continued to grow—along with his confusion. Why had she blown a gasket? After all, he'd just been playing poker with some of the guys he'd met at the wedding, not playing around with some little flirt.

He knew lots of men who took any opportunity to cheat on their wives, claiming that marriage hemmed them in, and that they needed something besides the "same old piece of stale cake" to get their adrenaline flowing.

But he wasn't like that. And he certainly didn't feel that way about his marriage.

The moment that he had first laid eyes on Claire in that cute little sundress she'd been wearing the day they met, peering into the show window of the furniture store where he worked, he had fallen for her like the proverbial ton of bricks. He'd even taken the initiative and gone outside the store to tell her that the set she was looking at was on sale. It really wasn't. He'd made that up just to have an excuse to talk to her.

Had she actually wanted to buy that set, he would have had to come up with the difference out of his own pocket, but he was so taken with her, he would have done it and gladly. The way he saw it, it would have been more than worth it to him.

From that day forward, Claire Strickland had always been the only girl for him. He'd loved her so much, he'd been willing to wait until she graduated from college before they got married. In fact, he'd insisted on it. First the degree, then the ring. Because it was best for her, and he didn't want to be the reason she had dropped out of college. From the first moment he met her, it had always been about what was best for her. He felt that she brought out the best in him.

And now he had lost her…and he wasn't even sure *why*.

He could still see that look on her face as she'd pushed him out of the room. She'd been so angry at him, and he hadn't done anything to warrant that degree of fury. One of the men in the game had actually bet and lost the house he was living in. Now *that* was stupid.

What would have been her reaction if he'd done something like *that*?

Trying to be optimistic, Levi had hoped that whatever had gotten her angry to this degree would blow over once they got back home.

But when they *did* get back home—she'd had her grandmother drive her and Bekka home while he'd driven himself—he'd found that his belongings had all been thrown out on the lawn in front of their apartment.

This, in addition to having thrown her wedding ring at him, made the message clear.

It was over.

Except that he didn't want it to be.

Desperate, thinking that maybe she needed a little bit of time to come around, he gave Claire her space. By definition, that required his staying out of her way, so he'd bedded down in the storeroom at the furniture store. He alternated between that and spending the night in his truck. It was August so at least he didn't have to worry about cold weather. But that was small consolation in the face of what was going on in his life.

With each passing day, he kept hoping that Claire would relent and take him back. But she never came to the store, never answered the phone when he called, even though he called her at least three times a day, if not more. For all intents and purposes, Claire was acting as if he didn't exist.

And it was killing him.

Frustrated, Levi decided that enough was enough and went to the apartment where they'd lived for the past two years for a face-to-face confrontation with Claire.

But as he drove up, he saw that there were no lights on in the window to greet him, and he had a very uneasy feeling as he unlocked the front door.

Holding his breath, praying he was wrong, Levi cautiously walked in.

"Claire? Claire, it's me. Levi. Your husband," he added uncertainly. Nothing but silence answered him. "Claire," he called out, "where are you?"

Still nothing. Nothing but the hollow echo of his own voice.

Growing progressively more agitated as well as aggravated, Levi went from room to small room, looking for his wife, for his baby. Finding neither.

"Come on, Claire, this isn't funny anymore. Where *are* you?"

Nervous now, he debated calling Claire's parents. He didn't want to worry them, but then on the other hand, there might be a chance that they knew where their daughter and granddaughter were.

They might even be staying with her parents, for that matter.

He took out his cell phone and was all set to press the appropriate numbers on the keypad, but then he paused, thinking. Maybe calling her parents wasn't such a good idea after all.

Claire's parents, Peter and Donna Strickland, had initially been very hesitant about their daughter getting involved with someone who was several years older than she was and who didn't have a college education. It had taken him a bit of doing to win them over.

But after her parents saw how much he really loved their youngest daughter, how he'd treated her as if she were made out of pure spun gold, they came around and gave their blessings. The older couple, who had been going strong for the past thirty years, had one of those rare, really happy marriages and according to Peter Strickland, they saw no reason why Claire and he couldn't have one, too.

If he called them, asking after Claire, then her parents would realize that they were having marital problems. He had a feeling that Claire *wouldn't* tell her parents what was going on. Because if she did, it was as good as admitting that their initial concerns about her getting married had been right. That he *wasn't* good enough for her. And even though she might actually believe that, he knew Claire well enough to know that she wouldn't readily admit that fact to her parents.

Who did that leave? he thought as he wandered around the empty apartment.

There were her two older sisters, Hadley and Tessa, but they were both professional career women who lived and worked in Bozeman, Montana, too. If Claire called either one of them, asking to be taken in, that would be as good as admitting failure, and she wouldn't do that. There was just the slightest bit of competitiveness among the sisters—at least as far as Claire was concerned.

No, she wouldn't call either one of her sisters, either. She would have rather died than allow her sisters to know that her marriage was in jeopardy.

But she had to call somebody, Levi reasoned. Claire couldn't opt to go it alone. She had the baby to think of.

The answer suddenly came to him. Of course. Claire would have turned to her grandparents for emotional support.

Her grandmother, Melba, was a lively, full-steam-ahead woman who had raised four children, including Claire's father, and had still managed to be a business-woman. She and her husband, Gene, ran the Strickland Boarding House, where he and Claire had stayed when they'd attended the wedding that had ultimately torn them apart.

Claire admired her grandmother, so it was only natural that she would turn to the older woman. And, as he recalled, the crusty Gene Strickland really doted on his granddaughter and her baby girl, too.

Levi was by nature a private person. He had never gone to anyone with his hat in his hand before, pleading his case, but then, he'd never been in this sort of a situation before, either. He wanted his wife and his daughter back in the worst way. Getting them back meant more to him than his pride, even though the latter was a difficult thing for him to swallow.

But he'd do it. To get Claire back into his life, he'd do whatever was necessary.

Levi slowly looked around the apartment. Claire's clothes were gone. The closets were empty on her side.

He knew that since Claire *was* gone, he could stay here again. The familiar surroundings were infinitely more comfortable than bedding down in the storeroom or utilizing the flatbed of his truck.

But staying here wasn't going to get him any closer to Claire. He needed to go into work every day—taking any more time off was out of the question since the store was introducing a new line of furniture and he was needed to handle whatever problems might come up. That meant that in his off hours, he needed to maintain close proximity to Claire. So he needed to stay somewhere close by to where she was staying.

And that, he concluded, would most likely have to

be at the boarding house. There'd been a couple of vacancies there last month when they were there for that damn wedding.

And even if there hadn't been, her grandfather was the type to find a way to make room for his granddaughter and his great-granddaughter even if it meant that *he* had to go sleep in his car. Gene Strickland would have thought nothing of it if doing so meant helping out Claire.

He needed to go see her grandparents, Levi decided. Her grandmother wasn't exactly a fan of his—the woman had made no bones about telling him that she thought Claire was too young to get married the first time she met him. But he did get along with Gene. If he could win the man over to his side in this, he'd have a fighting chance of winning Claire back, he reasoned.

Taking one last long look around, Levi closed and locked the front door behind him—fervently hoping that it wasn't for the last time.

How had she gone from feeling like a fairy-tale princess to being Cinderella before the fairy godmother had come into the picture in such a short amount of time?

Claire asked herself that question for the umpteenth time since she had come to her grandparents, asking if she could move into the boarding house until she could get on her feet again.

She could remember the way her grandmother had looked at her that day. Melba Strickland had never been what could be called a sentimental woman by any stretch of the imagination. But the woman was fair and she was family, which was what Claire felt she needed at a time like this.

At the time, her grandfather, a somewhat crusty bear of a man, had asked her, "What's wrong with your place?"

That was where she had broken down and cried. "I don't have a place anymore, Grandpa. I've left Levi."

"Left him?" Taking the fussing Bekka into his own arms, Gene cooed a few syllables at the baby, calming her down, and then looked at his granddaughter incredulously. "Don't you just mean that you've had a lovers' spat?"

Claire shook her head, unable to speak for a moment. When she finally could, she showed the two her bare left ring finger and said, "No, not a *lovers' spat*, Grandpa. Levi and I are separated." She took a ragged breath, telling herself that saying the words didn't hurt—but it did. She felt as if a jagged knife had just ripped through her heart. "We're getting divorced."

"Now hold on there, that's a big word, honey," Gene had told her. "Do you know what it means?"

Melba had frowned at her husband, annoyed. "Of course she knows what it means." And then she turned toward her granddaughter. "What happened, Claire? Did he disrespect you?" Her expression suddenly darkened. "He didn't lay a hand on you, did he? Because if he did, your grandfather is going to kill him."

Claire had struggled to keep her sobs from surfacing. "No, he didn't lay a hand on me, Grandmother."

"Then what happened? Why are you divorcing him?" Melba had demanded in her no-nonsense tone.

But Claire just shook her head, waving away the question. She had no intentions of reiterating the incident. She knew she'd break down before she even got to the middle of the story.

"It doesn't matter what happened. We're getting divorced. It's over," she told her grandparents with finality, her voice catching at the end.

For a moment she thought she was going to burst into sobs, but she managed to get herself under control at the last second.

Melba shot her husband a knowing look that all but shouted, "I told you so."

"I *knew* you were too young to get married." Although it was a declaration, there had been no triumph in Melba's voice. "You haven't had a chance to live yet. After graduating college, you're supposed to sample life a little. Travel. Do things, not tie yourself down with a marriage and a baby." She looked at her granddaughter knowingly. "Neither one of you was ready for that, especially not you."

"Melba," Gene warned, giving her a look that told her to keep her piece.

As headstrong and independent as ever, Melba was not about to listen. Hands on her hips, the diminutive woman turned on her husband. "Don't *Melba* me, Gene. She *wasn't* ready."

The steely older woman looked at her granddaughter, then, after a moment, she enfolded the girl in her arms. Melba's intentions were obviously good, but it still made for a rather awkward moment.

"Oh, Claire," Melba said with a sigh, "you wound up setting yourself up. Marriage isn't some magical, happily-ever-after state. At best it's an ongoing work in progress."

"I'll say," Gene chuckled, his chest moving up and down with the deep rumble. It managed to entertain Bekka, who in turn gurgled her approval. "The first hundred years are the hardest, honey," he told his granddaughter with a twinkle in his eye. "After that it gets easier. But you have to invest the time."

Claire had sniffled then, doing her best not to cry. Doing her best to face the rest of her life stoically. "That's all water under the bridge, Grandpa. I threw Levi out." That had been two days ago. "It's over."

Melba's dark eyebrows drew together in a puzzled single line. "If you threw Levi out, what are you doing here?"

Claire shook her head. "Well, it's his apartment. I can't stay there now. Everywhere I look—the kitchen, the closet, our bedroom—I can see him. It's just too hard for me to take."

Gene had glanced over toward his wife as if he knew that Melba was obviously going to say something that would echo the voice of reason—and be utterly practical. But Claire didn't need *practical*. What she needed—rather desperately, if the look in her eyes was any gauge—was understanding.

In order to forestall his wife and whatever it was

that she was going to say, Gene quickly spoke up, trying to stop whatever words were going to come out of Melba's mouth.

"Claire-bear," he said, addressing his granddaughter by the nickname he'd given her when she was about a month old, "You can stay here as long as you like. As it so happens, we've got a couple of vacancies, and it's been a long time since your grandmother and I have heard the sound of little running feet."

"Bekka is only eight months old, Grandpa. She doesn't even walk yet, much less run," Claire reminded her grandfather.

What her daughter did do, almost all night long, was fuss and cry. Another reason that she felt so worn out, hemmed in and trapped, Claire thought, struggling not to be resentful.

Her hostile feelings were redirected toward her husband. If he had been there to share in the responsibility, if he would have taken his turn walking the floor with the baby, then she wouldn't have felt as exhausted and out of sorts as she did.

"But she will," Gene was telling her. "She will and when she does, we'll be there to make sure she doesn't hurt herself, won't we, Mel?" he said, turning toward his wife.

"Sure. And the boarding house will just run itself," Melba commented sarcastically.

Gene shook his head as he looked at his granddaughter. "Don't mind your grandmother. She always sees the downside of things. Me, I see the upside." He winked at Claire. "That's why our marriage works."

"That's why your grandfather is a cockeyed optimist," Melba corrected.

For the sake of peace, Gene ignored his wife's comment. Instead, he said to Claire, "Like I said, you can stay here as long as you like." He turned toward the staircase, still holding Bekka in his arms. "Come on, we'll get you and the princess here settled in."

"I'll pay for the room, Grandmother," Claire had said, looking over her shoulder at Melba.

"You'll do no such thing," Gene informed her. "Family doesn't pay."

"But family pitches in," Melba had interjected. "We'll find something for you to do here at the boarding house, Claire."

"Anything," Claire had offered.

"How's your cooking?" Melba asked her. "I need someone to pick up the slack when Gina is busy," she elaborated, referring to the cook she'd recently hired. "I'm giving having someone else handling the cooking a try. I've already got a lot to keep me busy."

"Anything but that," Claire had amended almost sheepishly. "I'm afraid I still haven't gotten the hang of cooking." And then she brightened. "But I can make beds," she volunteered.

"This is a boarding house, Claire, not a bed-and-breakfast. People here make their own beds," Melba informed her matter-of-factly.

"Don't worry," Gene had said, putting one arm

around his granddaughter's shoulders as he held his great-granddaughter against him with the other, "We'll come up with something for you to do until you find your way."

Claire had sighed then, leaning into him as she had done on so many occasions when she had been a little girl, growing up.

"I hope so, Grandpa," Claire said, doing her best to sound cheerful. "I really hope so."

Chapter Two

Gene Strickland tried to ignore it, but even after all these years of marriage, he hadn't found a way to go about things as if everything was all right when it wasn't. His wife's scowl—which was aimed directly at him and had been an ongoing thing now for the past two weeks—seemed to go clean down to the bone. There was no use pretending that it didn't.

So he didn't even try.

Pushing aside the monthly inventory he was in the process of updating in connection with the boarding house's current supplies, Gene asked, "Okay, woman. Out with it. What's got your panties all in a twist like this?"

Brooding dark brown eyes looked at him accusingly from across the large scarred oak desk they both shared in the corner room that served as an office.

"As if you don't know," she muttered under her breath, but clearly enough for Gene to hear.

"No, I don't know," he'd informed her. "I'd like to think that I'd have the good sense *not* to ask if I knew. I've been with you long enough to know that lots of things set you off and right now, I don't want to risk bringing up any of them."

Melba pursed her lips as her eyes held his. "You're coddling her."

"Her?" Gene echoed innocently.

"Yes, *her*. Claire," she finally said. "Don't play dumb with me," Melba warned. "You know damn well that I'm talking about our granddaughter, Gene."

Unable to properly focus on the inventory while his wife was talking, Gene put down his pen and shook his head. This whole thing with Claire had hit Melba hard, he thought. He had a feeling that his wife blamed herself for not speaking up more to change Claire's mind about marrying so young. Or, at the very least, getting Claire to wait another year or so before leaping into marriage. But they all knew that the young never listened to the old, he thought, resigned.

Melba needed to change her opinion about Claire's marriage as well.

Especially since he was going to have to let her in on a secret he would have rather not had to divulge. However, if Melba found out about this on her own—and she had a knack for doing that—then Claire and Levi's marriage might not be the only one in trouble.

"Claire's going through a really rough patch right now, Mel."

"I know that," the old woman snapped. "And she needs a backbone to get through it, not to be treated as if she was made out of spun glass and could break at any second. She *needs* to toughen up." The very thought of a fragile granddaughter exasperated Melba beyond words. "Her parents were just too soft on her. If it were me, I would have never given my permission for those two to get married two years ago."

"Two years ago she wasn't a minor anymore, Mel," Gene gently reminded her. "Legally, she could make her own decisions," the man pointed out.

Melba threw up her hands. "And look how great that turned out for her," she huffed.

Gene thought of the newest boarder he'd just taken in—without his wife's knowledge, certainly without her permission.

Time to lay some groundwork, he told himself.

"Story's not over yet, Mel. There's a second act coming. I just know it. Just remember," he told her, making eye contact with the woman he had slept beside for five decades, "not everyone has an iron resolve like you." Gene leaned over and kissed his wife's temple.

"Don't try to sweet-talk me into going soft, Gene Strickland," Melba snapped—but with less verve.

It was obvious that even that small a kiss had her lighting up in response. They had a connection, she and Gene. The kind that poets used to celebrate in their works. And spats or not, the warranty on that connection hadn't expired yet.

"I wouldn't dream of it," he told her with a straight face. "As a matter of fact, I'm appealing to the businesswoman in you."

Melba looked at her husband, somewhat confused. Where was all this going? "What's that supposed to mean?" she wanted to know.

"Well, you're a savvy businesswoman, aren't you, Mel?" he asked.

"I like to think so," she said guardedly, watching her husband as if she expected him to pull a rabbit out of a hat or something equally as predictable, yet at bottom, magical. "Okay, out with it. Just where are you going with this?"

He built the blocks up slowly. "Being a good businesswoman means that you like to make money, true?"

"Yes, yes, we already know this," she told her husband impatiently. Everyone knew she loved making money, loved the challenge of running the boarding house efficiently. Having half a dozen adults—or so— in one place presented a great many hurdles to clear. But so far she was managing to run the place very successfully. "Get to the point. Sometime before next Christmas would be nice."

He approached the heart of this matter cautiously, determined to set up a strong foundation first. "A good businesswoman wouldn't allow personal prejudices to get in the way of her making a good-size profit."

Though Gene had argued against it, Levi had insisted

on paying more than the usual going rate for the room. Most likely in an effort to appeal to the entrepreneur in Melba when she learned of his being there.

"A good-size profit," she repeated. "What are you getting us into, Gene?" she wanted to know, eyeing her husband suspiciously. Usually, she could rely on him to ultimately come through at the end of the day, doing nothing to jeopardize their way of life or their income. But he was making her nervous now with his vague innuendos. Just exactly what did the man have up his sleeve?

"Making money in what way?" she asked her husband when he didn't answer her question.

"By renting out the last available room in the boarding house for more than the usual rate," he told her with just a shade too much innocence to satisfy Melba.

"What are you trying to say, Gene? Come on, spit it out," she ordered. "Just who is it that you're renting out this last room to?" she demanded. And then, just before her husband could give her an answer, a look of horrified indignation washed over the older woman's features. "Oh no, you can't mean to tell me—"

Her voice had gone up so high that it completely vanished at its peak.

Wanting to get this out and then, hopefully, put to rest, Gene supplied the name that Melba seemed incapable of uttering.

"Levi. Claire's husband. Yes, I rented it out to him," he told her with an air of finality that let her know that she was not allowed to toss the young man out on his ear under *any* circumstances.

Melba glared at him. "Have you gone and lost your mind, Gene?"

The heated accusation did *not* surprise him. "Not that I know of, no. Last I checked, it was still where it was supposed to be. Right between my ears—same as yours, Mel."

"Then why aren't you using it?" Melba wanted to know. Because the man was certainly acting as if he had lost his mind.

"I thought I was," he told her simply. "Not to mention my heart," he added pointedly.

"Claire came here to get away from that man," Melba reminded her husband. "Or did you somehow forget that little fact?"

"No, I didn't forget that," he replied calmly. "And since when did you condone cowardice?" Gene wanted to know.

The accusation instantly stirred her up. "What are you talking about?" Melba demanded heatedly. "I am most certainly *not* condoning cowardice."

He gave her a skeptical look. "Then what would you call letting her run away from her situation instead of facing up to it and trying to resolve it?"

Melba's scowl deepened, even though it didn't seem physically possible for it to become any deeper than it already was. She debated giving her husband the silent treatment, but the words were burning on her tongue, and she knew she'd have no peace until this was re-

solved and she said what had been—and still was—
on her mind.

"You and I both know that she married too young,"
she said to Gene.

Gene gave her a knowing look. "As I recall, she was
the same age as you were when we got married." Apparently, that little fact had escaped his wife.

"Don't compare us," Melba retorted. "I was years
older emotionally."

He tended to agree with her—although there were
times when he felt Melba was too young to make com-
petent decisions even at this age. Not that he would ever
dare to tell her that.

"Be that as it may," Gene told her, "Levi's a good
man, Mel, and he loves her." It was clear that he believed
the couple should take another shot at recapturing the
magic that had brought them together and had existed
in the first months of their marriage.

"Love alone never solved anything," Melba retorted.

Gene gave her a sly, knowing look. "Maybe not, but
it sure gave us something to look forward to on those
cold, long nights. Remember?"

Melba pressed her lips together and swatted her husband's arm. She could feel her cheeks warming. "Behave yourself, Gene."

Gene chuckled, amused. "You don't really mean that
and you know it," he told her.

The impish, sexy look he gave her melted the years
away and brought them both back to a time when the

only aches they felt involved their hearts and striving to be together over her parents' wishes otherwise.

Rising from his side of the desk, he circled around to where his wife was sitting. Hands bracketing her shoulders, he brought her up to her feet before him. Melba was a small woman. Her bombastic personality made him forget that at times. In reality, Gene all but dwarfed her when he stood beside his wife.

Height difference notwithstanding, Melba filled up his whole world and had from the moment he'd first met her.

"Give him a chance, Mel," he requested. "Give *them both* a chance to work this out."

Melba thought of how hurt Claire had been when she first came to them. How hurt she still seemed to be. "And if she doesn't want to?" she challenged.

"I have a feeling that she does," Gene told her confidently. He saw the skeptical look come over her face and said, "They have a daughter and four years invested in one another, two of them as a married couple. They've simply run into some turbulence just like a lot of other couples, but abandoning ship isn't the answer. If they do, if they don't try to make this work, they'll never forgive each other—or themselves."

Melba frowned, looking at her husband as if for the first time. "Since when did you get to be such a hopeless romantic?" she wanted to know.

That was an easy one to answer. "Since I married the most beautiful girl at the dance," he told her.

Melba huffed and shook her head. Her husband's answer both surprised her and pleased her, but she couldn't let him see that. If she did, she felt that she'd lose the upper hand in their relationship.

"Fine, Levi can stay," she informed him. "But he pays rent like everyone else," she warned. This wasn't a charity mission she was running here, she thought.

Levi had been one step ahead of Melba, Gene now thought. Insisting on paying more than the usual rate had been very smart of him. "I told you, that was already part of the deal."

Melba looked far from pleased. The scowl on her face not only remained, it deepened, too. "One wrong move and he's out of here."

"Understood." Gene paused, allowing her to savor her moment before he decided to bedevil her a little and asked, "Define *wrong move*."

She was at a disadvantage and not thinking as clearly as she should, Melba realized. Her mind was already on other matters that concerned the boarding house.

She chose the vague way out.

"You'll know it when you see it," she snapped. "Now I have to see if Gina has gotten dinner started," she told him, referring to the boarding-house cook. To that end, Melba shrugged off her husband's large, capable hands from about her shoulders. "One wrong move," she repeated warningly just before she left the room.

"Hard to believe that woman once had what I took to be a soft heart underneath all that," Gene said out loud to the other occupant of the area once his wife had left the room.

Turning around he looked at the young man he knew had been standing in the shadows of the hallway until the matter of his staying at the boarding house had been resolved. He was a little bit afraid of Melba—as were they all.

"But she does," Gene affirmed.

Levi looked off in the direction the woman had gone in. "She doesn't like me very much, does she?"

It wasn't a question so much as an observation on Levi's part.

"She likes you fine, boy," Gene assured him. "What she doesn't like is the situation. She's very protective of the people she loves, kind of like a lioness guarding her cubs. And there is no second-guessing her moves." He looked pointedly at his granddaughter's husband. "Consider yourself warned."

Levi nodded. "Yes, sir. And I appreciate you taking my side in this," he said with genuine gratitude and feeling.

"Not taking sides," Gene corrected the younger man. "Just facilitating things so that they can move ahead if that's what's in the cards. I think that little girl loves you," Gene told the young man who had come to him with his hat in his hand as well as his heart on his sleeve. "The problem is that she just got really overwhelmed by everything.

"People figure that getting married and having babies is no big deal—but it is. It's a *huge* deal, and there's a lot of adjusting to be done by everybody. You impress me as a sensible, hardworking young man, and I can tell that you love Claire—just like I can tell that she loves you. But she expected that life would go on being one great big party, and that's just not so. Marriage takes work and sacrifice. That's the part people forget about. If you find someone you love, there always comes a time when you have to fight for them. And that's a good thing in the long run because nothing that's precious gets that way if it's too easy."

Levi nodded. "I'm willing to fight for Claire until my dying breath."

"Nobody's talking about dying, boy," Gene told him, clapping one hand against Levi's broad shoulders. "Now come with me. I've got some things in the basement I need moved around and brought up to the kitchen. I could use a hand with them."

"Absolutely," Levi responded eagerly, wanting nothing more than to try to pay the man back in some small way for his kindness in allowing him this chance to win back the only woman he had ever loved.

Not a day went by when Claire didn't regret all the hot words that just seemed to fly out of her mouth on their own accord that fateful morning after the wedding reception. Most of all, she regretted throwing Levi out—and throwing her wedding ring at him. But she had been so angry and so hurt that he had preferred a stupid card game to being with her, she'd lost all reason. She'd been so furious, she was almost blinded by it.

At first she'd been so angry, she felt justified in leaving his phone calls unanswered.

But then he'd stopped calling.

Which meant to her that he had stopped caring. Because if Levi cared, he would have upped the number of his calls, not stopped them so abruptly. If he cared about her, truly cared, he would have come looking for her and wouldn't have stopped—not to eat or drink or sleep—until he found her. And then he would have gone on to move heaven and earth to win her back.

Since none of that, heretofore, had happened, nor did it appear to be happening, it just told her that she was right.

Levi *didn't* care anymore.

Well, if he didn't care anymore, then she didn't, either.

Except that she did.

She cared so much, she literally hurt inside. Which just served to make her feel as if she was a fool. Only a fool pined for someone who wasn't worth it, she argued over and over again.

What she needed to do, she told herself at least once a day, was to forget all about Levi and just move on, the way normal people did.

But how could she forget about him when every time she looked down into her daughter's face, she saw traces of Levi?

How could she move on when every morning began with thoughts of Levi? And every night ended that way, as well?

How could she forget about Levi when, in her head, she kept hearing his voice? Seeing his face? Everywhere she turned, she could swear he'd been there, or even *was* there.

She felt haunted, and with each day it was just getting worse, not better.

"Okay, today is the first day of the rest of your life, and you are going to stop this," Claire ordered her reflection in the mirror over the bureau. "You are going to take your adorable baby and march right out that door and into the rest of your life. A life without boundaries and without Levi."

Easier said than done, a little voice said in her head.

Still, she couldn't just live her life standing here in this room, staring at her reflection, too afraid to venture out.

"The hell I am," she declared out loud with enthusiasm.

So resolved, she took her baby daughter into her arms, rested Bekka on her hip and walked out of her room and into the rest of her life, or so she wanted to believe.

Unfortunately, as she all but marched into the hallway, she also walked straight into the person she was trying most to avoid.

She walked straight into Levi.

Chapter Three

Caught completely off guard, Claire shrieked.

Her breath caught in her throat as she felt her heart—an organ she had become painfully aware of in the past month—slam against her rib cage.

Stunned, she blinked, fully expecting Levi to fade away, a mere wistful product of her overactive imagination.

He didn't fade away. Levi remained exactly where he was, standing in front of her, holding on to her shoulders to keep her from falling.

He'd been hoping to run into her, but not quite like this and definitely not so literally.

Reacting automatically, Levi had grabbed his wife by the shoulders to steady her. That turned out to be a good thing, seeing how if he hadn't, Claire would have

probably stumbled backward and fallen while still holding Bekka tightly against her.

Holding on to Claire like this did more than just
prevent a very unfortunate accident from happening.
The exceedingly brief contact once again brought home
the fact that he'd missed her. Missed his wife acutely.
Missed the sight of her, the *feel* of her. The very first
time he'd laid eyes on her, he'd *known*. Known that
Claire Strickland was the one for him. Known that there
was something very special going on between them.

The chemistry that all but sizzled whenever they
were close to one another was just too hard to miss and
too intense to ignore. At that moment he'd realized that
he would have rather waited forever for Claire than settled for anyone else, no matter how willing she might
have been to be in a relationship with him.

Claire was completely shaken. It took everything she
had not to visibly tremble. Ever since she had thrown
her husband out of her life, her nights had been filled
with Levi.

Filled with dreams of him, with memories of him.

Filled with overwhelming longing for him.

In the privacy of the room she and Bekka were living in, she'd allowed herself to cry over a precious relationship that she believed in her heart had died—and
it was her fault.

Bumping into Levi like this, in the last place in the
world she'd thought that she would see him, her first
reaction was a surge of sheer joy, not to mention that
every fiber of her being had instantly—physically—

responded to the very sight of him. At that moment she would have thrown her arms around Levi's neck if her arms had been free.

The next moment her sanity, as she chose to view it, returned.

Luckily for her, she realized, her arms were filled with baby, so she couldn't go with her first impulse. That allowed her second impulse to take root and swiftly take over. Her second impulse belonged to the young woman who had felt hurt and abandoned that fateful night a month ago. It belonged to the young woman whose husband was absent a good deal of the time—not to mention that the one time he wasn't absent, he'd turned his back on her, choosing a stupid poker game over her company. That made the whole thing even worse because he'd abandoned her without so much as a second thought, as if she were some inconsequential afterthought in his life.

As that realization had taken root, Claire felt that she had to be worthless and unattractive in his eyes. This despite the fact that she had *always* made sure that she was her most attractive before he laid eyes on her in the morning. Even before she'd said "I do" she was determined not to turn into one of those wives who allowed herself to let her appearance go after the wedding.

To that end, Claire made sure that she was always up before Levi so that she could put on her makeup and be flawlessly beautiful when her husband looked at her first thing in the morning.

It wasn't always easy, but she'd managed. Her

makeup was flawless. The same went for her hair. Not a single strand was out of place, despite the demands of motherhood, made that much more acute by a colicky baby.

Claire's first priority was to make sure that she was just as attractive to her husband on an everyday basis as she had been the first time he'd seen her.

And where had that gotten her? Abandoned for the first night they'd had baby-free in eight months, that's where, she thought angrily.

The honeymoon, Claire thought not for the first time, was definitely over and so was, by default, their marriage.

Claire pressed her lips together, suppressing a sob. She just wished she didn't still want Levi so damn much. Levi was a fantastic, thoughtful lover. She had no need to go through a litany of others to know just how very special he was. Her heart—and her body—told her so.

But even so, she refused to allow herself to be a needy woman in that respect.

Refused to allow Levi to see the advantage he had over her.

Finally finding her voice, she demanded, "What are you doing here?" as she shrugged out of his grasp.

The second he was sure that Claire was steady on her feet, he dropped his hands from her shoulders. Making eye contact with his daughter, he winked at her.

Placing her hand so that she blocked the baby's line

of vision, Claire turned so that Bekka was against her and not between them.

Levi squelched the protest that rose to his lips. The only way he was going to get Claire back was not to antagonize her any further. That entailed walking on eggshells, but, seeing what was at stake, he was up to it. He had to be.

"I'm staying here for a while," he told her.

Claire's eyes widened in disbelief. Levi had never lied to her before—but he had to be lying now. There was no other explanation for what he had just said.

"No, you're not," she cried. Why was he messing with her mind like this? Wasn't it enough that he had ripped her heart right out of her chest?

"Yes, I am," he contradicted. "I convinced your grandfather to rent a room to me."

Claire felt as if someone had just literally yanked a rug out from under her feet and sent her crashing down to the floor.

Her grandfather wouldn't do that to her—would he? As early as this morning, she would have confidently maintained that her grandfather wouldn't rent Levi a room because he knew how much it would upset her— not to mention that allowing Levi to stay at the boarding house would effectively negate the very reason she was staying here instead of in the two-bedroom apartment that she had shared with Levi.

But now, looking at the confident expression on her estranged husband's face, she no longer knew if what he was telling her was a pack of lies—or actually the truth.

The look in her eyes dared him to continue with what she viewed as his fabrication. "Why would my grandfather do that?" she demanded.

It took everything Levi had in him not to just sweep her into his arms and kiss her, baby and all. But he knew he couldn't force this. For now he had to be satisfied with giving her his most sincere look as he pleaded his case, laying it at her feet. "Maybe your grandfather sees how much you mean to me."

Was he still doing this? Still perpetuating the lie he had tried to sell her in the wee hours of the morning when he had come stumbling in after the wedding reception had long been over? She was no more inclined to believe him now than she had been then.

Less, in fact.

There was no way she was going to let Levi think that she bought his story.

"Ha! If I meant anything to you, you'd be around more often, not working at all hours, going out of town for so-called meetings at the drop of a hat and going off to play poker when we were supposed to be spending time together on our first free night in months."

"We *were* spending time together," Levi insisted. "We went to the wedding together."

How gullible did he think she was? "*I* was in a room with a crying baby while *you* were at a poker table surrounded by your friends and playing cards until dawn. Just how is that being *together*?" Claire demanded hotly. Bekka began to fuss, and Claire automatically started to rock the baby to try and soothe her.

"Okay," Levi conceded. "But up to that point, we were together," he reminded her.

Stressed out, Claire began to pat the baby's bottom, trying desperately to calm her down.

"That *was* the whole point," she informed Levi. "After the wedding we were supposed to spend some quality time together," she insisted. "My grandparents were taking care of Bekka. You and I were supposed to spend a nice, romantic evening together."

"How was I to know that? You didn't tell me," Levi pointed out.

Claire stared at him, stunned. He couldn't have been that thickheaded—could he?

"I shouldn't *have* to tell you," she cried. "You're supposed to have *wanted* that on your own, not had me force-feed you your lines or hold up a cue card for you."

The only way he could think to backtrack out of the potential explosion in the making he saw coming was to apologize. So he gave it a shot.

"Look, if I messed up, I'm sorry—"

"If? *If?*" Claire echoed incredulously. "You most certainly *did* mess up, no *if* about it."

She was getting him exasperated again, hitting the ball totally into his yard and then not allowing him to retrieve it or hit it back. He should have expected as much, he thought.

Mentally, Levi counted to ten, telling himself that he had to be calm or he would wind up losing any chance he had to get Claire back.

To get Bekka back.

He missed them both like crazy.

"Claire," he said as evenly as possible, "I'm trying to apologize here."

Her eyes were like small, intense laser beams, trained on his every move. "I'm glad you told me because I wouldn't have known otherwise," she informed him.

"You're making it really hard to be nice to you," he told her, his anger getting the best of him, at least for the moment.

"Then don't bother," Claire snapped coldly. She was forced to raise her voice because Bekka had started to wail again. The increased volume only made the baby cry more. "Because it's not going to get you anywhere. Apologies have to be sincere, and I can see now that every single word out of your mouth is nothing but a fabrication, a lie."

"What are you talking about?" Levi cried, completely confused. "When have I lied to you?"

Claire tossed her head, wanting desperately to get away from him and wanting, just as desperately, to never have gotten to this point in the first place. This wasn't the way she envisioned her life when she'd watched Levi slip the ring on her finger two years ago.

"You said you loved me," she accused.

"How is that a lie?" he wanted to know. "I *do* love you."

"No, you don't!" Claire cried. "If you loved me, you'd be home more often at night and you certainly wouldn't have picked poker over me."

He closed his eyes, searching for strength. How did

he get through to her? "That again," he retorted. "I didn't pick poker over you—"

"Oh, someone put a gun to your head then, telling you to deal or they'd blow your brains out, is that it?"

"It wasn't a choice between you and poker," Levi insisted. How could she possibly think that? "You're not in the same league."

Was that supposed to make her happy? Claire looked at her husband coldly, doing her very best not to allow her mind to drift, to make her think back and relive exciting, intimate moments with him just because of their proximity. "Thanks."

Her icy tone ripped through him, and Levi threw up his hands in total disgust. "I just can't win with you, can I?"

"No, because I see right through you," she informed him, her voice cold enough to freeze a cup of hot coffee. Just then, as if she was aware that she had lapsed into another long, quiet moment, the baby began to cry. "Now look what you've done. You've agitated the baby," she accused.

"Me?" he said, stunned at the way she could shift blame onto someone else's shoulders so easily. "You're the one who's shouting."

Claire made no effort to back down or back off. The baby grew louder with each passing second. "If I'm shouting it's so I can get the words through your thick skull."

He sighed, shaking his head and struggling not to have his temper snap. "You're impossible."

"Right back at you!" she retorted.

Levi strode away before he said something he was going to regret and couldn't take back.

"That's right," she taunted, hurling the words at his back. "Run. That's all you ever do. You're never willing to talk things out, to own your mistakes. It's just easier for you to run away from any confrontation."

Don't say it, don't say it, Levi counseled himself, afraid that if he did open his mouth, he wouldn't be able to control the words that would come flying out. There was no doubt about it. Claire knew how to press all his buttons. Press them until he believed that all the negative thoughts she was spouting and hurling at him were his own, and all the detrimental things that Claire had said against him she actually believed to be the gospel truth.

There was a child to think of, Levi reminded himself. He couldn't just put this all behind him and walk out. Besides, he didn't *want* to. What he wanted was his life back.

Not today, Wyatt. Not after that little run-in, a voice in his head mocked him.

But where did that leave them?

They were at an impasse, he thought. But one of them was going to have to give in if this was ever going to be resolved.

Walking away, Levi paused for a second to look over his shoulder at his wife and daughter. Even as angry as she made him, he couldn't help thinking how much he'd missed having them in his life.

How empty his life seemed with the realization that he didn't have them to come home to anymore.

That had to change.

But how?

He wasn't about to come crawling over to her side. After all, a man did have his pride.

But pride was a cold thing to take to bed with him, Levi thought unhappily.

Besides, there had to be more to this. She couldn't be this angry over a stupid poker game—could she? He needed to get her to do more than just shout at him. He had to get her to come around—and really talk to him about what she was feeling,

Squelching the desire to march back to her, take her into his arms and kiss her until she forgot all about this stupid argument and all the stupid things she was saying to him, Levi forced himself to keep walking.

This was all probably just a ruse on her part anyway. Her so-called accusations were just an excuse she was using to stay away from him because she was disappointed in him.

He'd failed her somehow, and by failing he'd inadvertently shown her that he just wasn't good enough for her. That he couldn't give her the kind of comforts she had grown up with. Even if he tried to approximate the kind of life she'd had before she married him by working his way up the ladder and earning more money, she complained that he was never home. And if he kept the hours that she wanted him to, if he was home earlier,

then he couldn't give her any of the things she'd come
to expect in her day-to-day life.

Either way, Levi thought glumly, he was doomed.

He had to get his priorities straight. He needed to
find a way to fix all this and soon, otherwise, he was
going to lose her for good.

Levi didn't know how much longer he could put up
with living without his girls. Living without seeing
Claire and Bekka every day.

There *had* to be a way to fix all this. There just *had*
to be.

"Grandpa, can I see you for a minute?" Claire asked,
standing in the doorway of Gene's cubbyhole of an office.

Gene rose to his feet. For the time being, what he
was working on was temporarily forgotten.

"You, princess, can see me for a whole hour if you
like," he told her cheerfully. Joining them, he asked,
"And how are my two best girls this morning?"

Claire thought of her run-in with Levi a few minutes
ago. "Stunned and confused," she told him.

Bushy eyebrows drew together, forming a squiggly
line worthy of a fat caterpillar.

"Come again?" Gene asked. "Are you stunned and
confused, peanut?" he asked Bekka.

Responding to the sound of his deep, resonant voice,
the baby cooed at Gene, making him laugh with un-
abashed pleasure.

"Grandpa, she can't talk," Claire informed the older
man flatly.

"Maybe you can't understand her, but she can talk," he assured Claire with a touch of whimsy. "Look at her expression," he said pointedly. "That little girl is definitely trying to communicate."

"And so am I," Claire said to her grandfather in barely curbed exasperation.

Faced with this situation, Gene sobered slightly. "Go ahead, princess. I'm listening."

Claire's frown deepened. "Levi is staying here at the boarding house."

He had a feeling that Claire knew she wasn't telling him anything that he wasn't already aware of. He didn't bother feigning surprise at her news.

"Yes, I know."

She stared at the older man in disbelief. How could he have betrayed her this way? Unless Levi was lying about this, too. She found herself fervently hoping that he was. Otherwise, this was really going to shake her faith in her grandfather.

"He said you rented him a room." Maybe there was some other explanation for his being here.

The next moment her grandfather dashed that slim hope. He nodded his head. "I did."

Her mouth all but dropped open. "Why?" Claire demanded.

"Well, I couldn't very well not rent it to him," Gene replied seriously. "That would be prejudicial."

Claire's big brown eyes widened. She couldn't believe her ears. "Are you saying you were afraid he'd report you to the sheriff?"

Wide shoulders moved up and down in a vague shrug. He went with the excuse his granddaughter had unknowingly come up with.

"You never know," he told her.

"Grandpa, this is Levi," she reminded him. "He wouldn't do that. Levi *likes* you."

"He also likes you," Gene told her. "A *lot*. And all he wants is a chance to prove it."

Claire couldn't believe her ears. "You're taking his side, Grandpa?" she cried, appalled.

"Like I told your grandmother, I'm not taking any sides, I'm just making sure that both sides get a chance to be heard."

"I don't need to 'hear' anything," his granddaughter informed him. "Besides," she reminded the man, "weren't you the one who once told me that actions speak louder than words?"

"I might have said that," he allowed, then went on to remind her, "I'm also the one who said everyone deserves a second chance."

"If you mean Levi, I *gave* him a second chance." She was working herself up. "I gave him *lots* of second chances, and he blew them all."

"He's been skipping out on you to play poker on a regular basis?" Gene asked innocently.

"No," she admitted reluctantly. As upset as she was about this situation, she wasn't about to lie about it to her grandfather.

Her grandfather looked at her pointedly. "Then what?" he wanted to know.

She was referring to Levi going out of town for meetings and seminars as well as coming home late and falling asleep on the couch before she could get his dinner warmed up. But she had no intentions of going into all that now.

Besides, she had a feeling that her grandfather would be taking Levi's side in that, saying he saw nothing wrong in a man trying to better his family's lot by putting in all those long hours at work.

"I don't want to talk about it," she informed her grandfather and with that, she turned on her heel and hurried away to find her grandmother.

At least her grandmother sided with her, Claire thought.

Or at least she hoped so.

Chapter Four

Holding a fussing Bekka in her arms, Claire went in search of her grandmother. Between feeling betrayed by her grandfather and being subjected to her baby's incessant crying, her nerves felt as if they were stretched as far as they could go. She was beyond stressed out.

"Come on, Bekka. Please stop," she begged.

Bekka went on crying.

At her wit's end, Claire finally found the object of her search in the kitchen. Melba was going over a menu change with the cook. Gina tapped the older woman on the shoulder and pointed behind her.

The moment she realized that her granddaughter was there, Melba paused, telling the cook, "We'll talk later." With that, she waited for Claire to join her.

"Is it true?" Claire asked without any preamble.

"Is *what* truc?" Melba wanted to know, peering over the tops of her rimless glasses at her distressed granddaughter. And then she smiled, tickling Bekka under her chin. "Hi, peanut," she cooed.

"I just found out that Grandpa rented out Jordyn Leigh's old room to Levi," Claire complained, referring to the young woman who'd moved out last month after marrying her longtime best friend, Will Clifton, a rancher from Thunder Canyon. They'd apparently tied the knot during the reception of the wedding she and Levi had attended last month.

"Yes, I know," Melba replied matter-of-factly with a dismissive shrug. She wasn't exactly happy at inviting this turmoil onto her home turf, but maybe Gene was right. Maybe Levi should be given another chance to make things right between him and Claire. Her granddaughter certainly wasn't happy with the current state of her marriage.

Claire had come looking for sympathy. That her grandmother had had knowledge of this beforehand—and *hadn't* warned her—all but left her speechless.

It was all she could do not to have her jaw drop open.

"You *know*?" Claire cried, surprised. "Then it's actually all right with you?" She stared at her grandmother, dumbfounded.

Claire made no attempt to hide the fact that she felt deeply wounded by what she viewed as an act of betrayal. It didn't matter that she was having ambivalent feelings about throwing Levi out, that part of her was actually happy about this odd turn of events that was throwing her husband and her together. What mattered was that the rest of her was more than a little upset by the same set of circumstances. Her grandparents were supposed to be on her side; they were supposed to be protecting her, shielding her, not tossing her headfirst into the lion's den.

Levi had hurt her, and she didn't want him thinking that it was no big deal. Nor did she want him to think that all he had to do was turn up on her doorstep and she would forgive him.

The truth of it was that she wasn't sure *what* to feel, but because of what she had told her grandparents—that she'd left Levi because he neglected her and took her for granted—she felt that her grandparents were supposed to be supportive of her. They were supposed to present a united front and most certainly shun Levi because of the thoughtless way he had treated her. Whether or not he was paying them rent didn't change anything. They most certainly shouldn't have allowed Levi to take up residence in the very house where she was staying.

What were they *thinking*?

"I didn't say that," Melba pointed out calmly. "Your grandfather did what he did—renting the room out to Levi—without consulting me."

Claire immediately jumped on what she took to be the rightful implication. "Then you can overrule Grandpa on this, right?" she asked eagerly.

Having Levi here would just heighten her ambivalent feelings, making her go back and forth mentally like some sort of a virtual Ping-Pong ball. It would be for the best to have him leave here. She needed her space so she could make a decision about her future. She couldn't do that with Levi around. Seeing him only reminded her how much she wanted him to hold her, to kiss her, to— He had to go, she thought, agitated. If he didn't, she knew she was liable to do something very stupid.

"You can tell Levi that he's not welcomed here and has to get out," Claire concluded.

Melba gave her a reproving look. "You know I can't very well do that, Claire. According to your grandfather, Levi paid twice the going rate for a month in advance."

"Just give the money back to him," Claire insisted as if it was the simplest thing in the world. "Tell him he has to leave," she pleaded.

Melba gave her granddaughter a long, thoughtful look. "Claire, your grandfather happens to think that Levi deserves a second chance. And I happen to think that your grandfather usually displays good judgment, so he just might be right about your husband."

"Ex-husband," Claire corrected, exasperated. Why was everyone against her? It was hard enough steering clear of Levi. If he was on the same floor as she was, she was doomed.

Melba paused. "You're already divorced?"

Claire flushed as she struggled to quiet her baby. "Well, technically, no," she admitted, "but—"

Melba took the baby from her, patting the baby's bottom and murmuring something soothing into the tiny ear. As if by magic, Bekka began to settle down.

"Then *technically*, you are still married," Melba told

her, "which makes Levi your husband, not your ex-husband."

Claire blew out a breath, surrendering—temporarily. "Technically, yes," she conceded grudgingly, clinging to the word.

Melba studied her for a long moment. Claire was so different from her two older sisters. Those girls took after *her*, Melba thought. They were professionals, focused and driven, unlike Claire. She understood Hadley and Tessa. Claire was harder for her to read.

But she was trying. Lord knew she was trying.

"What are you afraid of, Claire?" Melba gently asked her granddaughter.

"Afraid of?" Claire repeated, somewhat confused by the question. "I'm not afraid of anything."

The more she thought about it, the more convinced Melba was that she was right. Claire was most definitely afraid of something. And she had a sneaky feeling she knew what.

"Oh, yes, you are. You're acting as if you're afraid of being in the same room with Levi. As if, if you remain around Levi, those walls you've built up against him are going to come crumbling down around you, allowing Levi to come back into your life."

Claire waved her grandmother's words away. Indignant and upset at her grandmother's assessment of her, she tossed her head. "You're just imagining things, Grandmother."

Melba's eyes met hers. "I am, am I? Well, if I am,

it doesn't really harm anything to have Levi here now, does it?"

Claire squared her shoulders. "I just don't want him around here," she insisted.

"Why?" The single word seemed to burrow straight into Claire.

She was used to being backed up and getting her way when it came to her family. Losing that crutch left her bewildered and at loose ends, not to mention very unsteady. "Because I don't," Claire stubbornly insisted.

The look Melba gave her made her fidget inside. Furthermore, she looked on with envy at the way her grandmother seemed to be able to quiet Bekka down with no effort at all.

"That's not a reason, Claire."

"It is for me," Claire maintained.

"Well, sadly for you, you don't run Strickland's Boarding House," Melba crisply informed her. "Your grandfather and I do. My advice to you is either make the best of this—or make yourself scarce whenever Levi comes around. By the way, your grandfather is putting that boy's strong back to use while he's here, so you'll be seeing him around a lot during the evening hours."

She couldn't have been on the receiving end of worse news. After a full day of boredom and longing, her resistance to Levi would have the strength of shredded, wet tissue paper.

"I thought you of all people would be on my side," Claire lamented.

"I *am* on your side, Claire," her grandmother informed her in her no-nonsense voice.

Claire knew she was pouting, but she couldn't help herself. "Doesn't feel that way to me."

Melba allowed a small sigh to escape. The girl had a lot of growing up to do, she thought.

"Someday, when you get to be around my age, you'll see that I was right and you'll thank me."

Claire's frown deepened by several degrees. She felt utterly abandoned and at a loss as to what to do and how to proceed. "If you say so," she said without any sort of enthusiasm.

Melba's eyes met her granddaughter's. "I do," the older woman said with conviction. "It's either that," her grandmother went on, "or admit that I was right in the first place."

At this point Claire was utterly confused as to what her grandmother was referring to. "Right about what?" she wanted to know.

"That you were too young and too immature to get married."

Her grandmother certainly didn't pull any punches, Claire thought, dismayed. Well, she wasn't about to admit that the woman was right about that, because she wasn't, Claire thought fiercely. About the only thing she was willing to admit at this point was that Levi had no idea how to treat a wife, how to make her feel loved, rather than inconsequential.

And everything else was beside the point as far as she was concerned.

It felt as if everyone was ganging up on her. There were tears gathering in her eyes, and she had to blink hard to keep them from sliding down her cheeks. She focused on making the tears go away.

Taking a defensive stance, Claire raised her chin pugnaciously. "I was the same age you were when you got married. Grandpa told me so," she added in case her grandmother was going to dispute the fact.

As if to prove that she was a good mother, Claire took the baby from her grandmother and back into her arms. The second she did, Bekka looked discontented. Within moments, she began to fuss again. Claire's heart sank. What *was* it that she was doing wrong?

Meanwhile, Melba looked entirely unaffected by the comparison that her granddaughter had brought up. "Only chronologically."

"Well, yes, chronologically," Claire agreed, clearly puzzled. Her grandmother was trying to confuse her, she thought. "What other way is there?"

"Emotionally," Melba readily answered. "At the time," she recalled, "I was a great deal older than you emotionally—*and* I was fully prepared to take on the responsibility of raising not just one child but eventually four of them—in short order. You can't say the same thing," Melba said with what Claire felt was unnerving certainty. "Raising one child seems to have confounded you."

Inwardly, Claire shuddered at the very mention of four babies. As much as she loved Bekka—and she loved her a great deal—the thought of two children, much less four, had her breaking out in a cold sweat.

She couldn't deny the fact that Bekka was proving to be hard enough for her to deal with. It seemed to her as if, ever since the baby had come into her life, she hadn't had a moment's peace or even a real moment to herself. Every minute of every day seemed to belong to Bekka. Even when the little girl was sleeping, Claire found herself waiting for the next go-round of crying and fussing to begin.

Or, at the very least, the next round of breast-feeding to get underway. Her only function seemed to be to serve the baby.

Claire felt as though she was being held prisoner by an eight-month-old. Even when, in those rare moments Bekka wasn't fussing, it was only a matter of time until she would begin again.

There was no denying that Claire felt as if she was on some giant, endless treadmill that was only moving faster and faster with each passing moment.

And she couldn't keep up.

Bekka was becoming more and more vocal—again. Why couldn't she get the baby to stop crying? Claire wondered with a barely suppressed ragged sigh.

"I guess it's time to go feed her again," she said, resigned.

But as she turned to go, Melba moved suddenly in order to get in front of her, her arms outstretched. "Why don't you let me take care of that?" she suggested then nodded toward the back porch. "Go get yourself some fresh air. Take a walk."

Claire didn't understand what her grandmother was saying. "Are you telling me that you're going to feed Bekka?"

Melba didn't see why her granddaughter looked so befuddled about this. "That's exactly what I'm telling you."

"How?" Claire wanted to know. "I'm breast-feeding her, Grandmother." She would have been willing to bet that it had been a very long time since the other woman had been in her position. "No offense, but you *can't* feed her."

"Yes, I can," Melba contradicted. Resting the baby on her hip, she went toward the refrigerator. Opening the door, she reached toward the shelf that had several bottles all prepared and lined up in a row. Claire could only stare at them. "I'll warm up some formula for the baby."

"Formula?" Claire echoed in surprise. They'd had this discussion earlier, and she had vetoed the idea. Apparently, her grandmother was every bit as headstrong as her grandfather had warned her that she was. "I thought we agreed that Bekka's too young for that."

"*You* agreed, I didn't. Bekka is the *perfect* age for that. What are you going to do?" Melba wanted to know. "Breast-feed that child until she's ready to go off to college?"

"No, of course not," Claire retorted, rolling her eyes at the ludicrous suggestion. "But—"

"No *but*," Melba said firmly, shutting her down. "I raised four children," she said, citing her credentials. "Each of them was on the bottle by the time they were six months old. If you ask me, Bekka's way overdue. You don't want her being socially arrested, now, do you?"

"No," Claire replied in a small voice, confusion reigning all through her. What did one thing have to do with the other? she wondered.

Melba looked at her granddaughter knowingly. "Then stop using the child as an excuse."

Further lost than ever now, Claire could only stare at her grandmother. "What do you mean as an excuse? I'm not using her as an excuse."

Melba saw it different. "Oh, yes, you are." And then she gave Claire an example. "'I know what you're thinking. You feel as though you can't make a move anywhere, can't go out of the house because your baby needs you 24/7." Melba gave her youngest granddaughter a knowing, penetrating look. "The truth is, she doesn't. And you *can* leave her side here and there for a bit. So do it," Melba encouraged. "While it's very true that a baby does shake up your life, there are still parts of that life that belong exclusively to you, so reclaim them. Now go. I've got a great-granddaughter to feed," she told Claire, shooing her granddaughter out of the kitchen with her one free hand.

Claire stopped short just beyond the entrance to the kitchen.

Except for the few hours that she and Levi had attended the wedding, Bekka had either been in her arms or within arm's reach since the day she was born. The baby's crib was set up in their bedroom and during her own waking hours, Claire carried the baby around with her almost everywhere. If she did set the child down, she was always close by at all times.

To have her arms empty like this and to have Bekka out of her line of sight felt very strange.

It also, heaven help her, felt liberating, Claire thought.

So she did as her grandmother had suggested. Leaving the boarding house, she took a walk around the area, keeping close by—just in case she was needed. Old habits were hard to break.

It was August, which meant that, for the most part, the weather was hot and humid—not unlike the summer that she had first met Levi, Claire caught herself nostalgically remembering.

No, don't do that. Don't get all sentimental on me now, she chided herself. *That's not going to help anything*.

Her head began to hurt.

Admittedly, Claire thought as she walked slowly around her grandparents' property, she was very confused about her situation. Part of her felt she'd been justified in the way she'd reacted to Levi's absences, and especially to that night after the reception.

That was the part of her that felt that there was no turning back from what she'd done, throwing him out like that. Levi was going to come to his senses, decide that he could do a lot better than to tie himself down to a woman who was, for all intents and purposes, a shrew who could only find fault with him rather than to be grateful for the virtues he displayed.

There wasn't a chance in hell that this was going to have the happy ending she was hoping for. Levi was definitely *not* going to want her back after the way she'd treated him.

He was probably here not to try to win her back, but to make her regret what she had done. Regret it and see what she had lost by tossing him out.

That meant that Levi was probably here out for revenge.

Her headache was getting worse.

Not only that, but it felt as if there really was this internal Ping-Pong game going on, and her feelings kept going back and forth like the ball being lobbed over the net.

In all honesty, she didn't know just which side of the net the ball really belonged.

She needed to get back, Claire told herself. The baby had been with her grandmother long enough. She couldn't just pass Bekka along as if she was some sort of a doll. She was a flesh-and-blood child.

Bekka was *her* responsibility, not her grandmother's or her grandfather's.

Holding Bekka in her arms—even when the baby insisted on fussing—was the only time that everything felt even marginally right, Claire thought.

Until she could figure her life out, she was going to hold off on making any major decisions.

She had spent enough time away from her baby, she told herself, quickening her pace.

When she got back into the kitchen, Claire found that neither her grandmother nor her baby were there. She quickly made her way around to the back of the house and exited through the rear door onto the porch.

Even as she began to push the door open, she heard the sound of voices.

One belonged to her grandmother, and the other voice—Claire cocked her head even as the answer came to her—belonged to Levi.

Moving quickly, Claire's first thought was to retrieve her baby. But even before she could reach Levi and Bekka, she could see that, instead of fussing and crying, the little girl was smiling and cooing.

There was some formula staining her dimples— dimples that the little girl had in common with her daddy, Claire thought ruefully. Despite Bekka's less than pristine appearance, she hadn't seen the baby looking this contented in more than a month—since the last time she had observed Levi and their daughter together.

He had a way with her, Claire admitted grudgingly.

Levi glanced up just as she approached them. He appeared to look just a tad sheepish, but he made no attempt to stop feeding the baby or to get up and surrender their daughter to her.

From out of nowhere, Melba came up directly behind her.

"They look good together, don't they?" her grandmother observed.

Claire fisted her hands at her sides as she turned toward the woman. "I thought you said you were going to feed her."

"I was, but then Levi came over and asked me if I'd mind if he held Bekka for a few minutes. A loving father shouldn't have to ask for permission to hold his own baby daughter," Melba told her, "so I let him take Bekka and feed her." Small brown eyes narrowed as she looked pointedly at her granddaughter. "Do you have a problem with that?"

"No, ma'am, I don't," Claire replied quietly.

"Good, because you shouldn't." She looked from Levi to Claire, making up her mind. "All right, since the two of you are here now, I'll leave my great-granddaughter in your so-called 'capable' hands—try not to argue around her. She might be too young to talk, but she's not too young to hear or to be affected by the sound of raised voices and misbegotten accusations," Melba informed them pointedly.

The next moment the woman turned on her stacked heel and walked away.

Chapter Five

Gently rocking his daughter in his arms as he continued feeding Bekka her bottle, Levi silently watched Melba Strickland walk away.

"Tough lady, your grandmother." There was admiration in his voice.

"Yes," Claire agreed. "Grandmother's been known to be tough as nails."

But Melba only held his attention for a moment. The little beauty in his arms had more than garnered the bulk of it. He could feel his heart swelling as he looked at her. They had been apart for thirty days. How much had he missed out on in thirty days?

He had a feeling that it was a lot. Every moment was precious at this point of his daughter's development. He didn't want to miss any more.

"I can't believe how much she's grown," Levi murmured, more to himself than to the woman standing near him.

Claire's attention had been focused on her grandmother and the fact that the woman was truly acting as if she saw nothing wrong with Levi invading the boarding house like this.

She turned now to look at Levi quizzically. "Grandmother?"

"No," he laughed. Lookswise, Claire's grandmother hadn't changed a hair since he'd first met her four years ago. "Bekka. She looks like she's beginning to really fill out. And there's personality in those eyes of hers. She's going to be a regular heartbreaker when she grows up." As she continued to suck enthusiastically on her bottle, Levi smiled down into his daughter's face. "I've missed you, little darlin'," he told her. "Did you miss me, too?"

More than anything in the world, Claire thought. observing the way he was with Bekka. *And more than you'll ever know.*

With more than a little effort, she blocked and shut down her feelings. She was *not* about to own up to what she was thinking or say the words out loud.

That was all she needed to do, Claire upbraided herself. If Levi had a clue as to what she was thinking, he would just take that to mean that he could move back into their apartment and just like that, it would be business as usual.

Would that be so bad? she questioned herself.

Yes! Yes, it would be that bad. She'd be back to

spending all of her time taking care of the baby and missing Levi while he'd be spending all his free time away from her.

Supposedly securing their future if she was to believe him.

She had to remember how that felt, missing him. Being taken for granted, she silently counseled herself.

But all that—staying angry—required effort. Effort that was hard to maintain when part of her kept longing for the touch of his hand, the feel of his lips on hers.

Seeing him with Bekka certainly didn't help.

Watching Levi with their infant daughter tugged at her heart in a way she'd never anticipated. The feeling sliced through her insecurities and her hurt.

It also did something else she hadn't anticipated.

It made her feel just the slightest bit jealous.

Her baby was responding to Levi the way she didn't to *her*. Bekka was cooing and making a host of other contented noises whereupon when she held Bekka, all the baby did was fuss and cry.

Maybe the baby really *was* picking up on her stress levels, Claire thought. But in that case, it also meant that Levi *wasn't* stressed in the least about their estranged situation.

And that, in turn, meant that he just didn't care about either.

If that was the case, why was she standing here, looking at him like some lovesick simpleton? Didn't she *know* any better by now?

Bekka was finally finished with her bottle. Setting it

aside, he put the baby over his shoulder and patted her back the way he had learned surfing YouTube videos that were meant for new dads.

"You should put something on your shoulder," Claire advised coolly. "She'll spit up on it."

"That's okay," he told her, making small, concentric circles on the baby's small back, intermittently patting it, as well. "The shirt's washable."

His heart swelled just holding his daughter like this. She felt so tiny, so dependent on him. So precious. He'd never thought that he could fall in love so quickly, so completely, and yet this little girl held his heart in the palm of her hand. He'd fallen in love with her even faster than he had fallen for her mother, he thought.

It went without saying that he would do anything for Bekka, anything to keep her safe and warm. And happy. He also didn't want to spend another day without her, much less another month.

There had to be a way.

Searching for a way to initiate "peace talks" with his estranged wife, he glanced up and saw a rather strange expression on Claire's face. One he couldn't really begin to read.

"What?" he asked.

Watching the way Bekka responded to Levi, she was beginning to feel threatened. And left out.

"I'd like my daughter back, please," Claire said primly as she reached for Bekka.

"*Our* daughter," Levi emphasized. "Bekka's *our* daughter."

She wasn't about to be lectured to by this absentee father. Not after all the lonely hours she'd put in, caring for Bekka by herself.

"Oh, so now she's *our* daughter, is she?" Claire demanded hotly.

"What are you talking about?" Levi asked. He could feel another fight brewing. Why did she insist on doing that? On picking fights when all he wanted to do was to make up and go from there? "She's always been our daughter."

She had her hands on Bekka, but Levi was still holding her. "Then why were you never around to help take care of her?"

"It wasn't *never*," he corrected defensively.

"Well, it certainly felt that way. Every time I could have used your help, you weren't there," she accused.

"That's because I was earning money to provide for Bekka *and* for you." Because he was afraid that Bekka could turn into the main component in a tug of war, he relinquished his hold on his daughter, albeit reluctantly. He would have been willing to hold her all day if he could.

Claire rested the baby against her shoulder while she glared at Levi. "Ah, yes. Saint Levi, working all those long hours to bring home a paycheck. Why is it that other fathers seem to be able to keep regular hours while you're gone from dawn to midnight, using any excuse not to come home?"

Now she was just making things up, Levi thought, frustrated. "That's not true and you know it," he told her, struggling not to raise his voice. He didn't want to make Bekka cry. "I got a promotion so I have to put in longer hours. I've got a lot of new responsibilities, as well as my old ones. If I start telling the boss I can't attend those meetings and seminars he keeps sending me to, he'll replace me with someone who can. Tell me, what good will I be doing Bekka or you if I can't pay for a roof over your heads?" he wanted to know.

He thought that would finally be the end of it—but he should have known better.

She narrowed her eyes as she looked at him. "At least we'd both know your face."

"Come on, Claire," he said in disbelief, "that's not fair."

"Fair?" she echoed incredulously. "I'll tell you what's *fair. Fair* is taking your turn walking the floor with a shrieking baby. *Fair* is taking turns changing her diaper, giving her a bath, watching out for her so she doesn't bump her head. *Fair* is giving me someone to talk to once in a while besides a fussing infant."

"Why don't you call your sisters, talk to them?" he suggested.

She could also just as easily have called her mother, but he had a feeling that her pride was keeping her from admitting to her mother that she found motherhood to be far more difficult to deal with than she'd thought—just as her mother had tried to get her to realize that it would be.

Claire was just too stubborn for her own good, he thought.

"What, you mean call them instead of you?" Claire asked in disbelief. "I love my sisters. But I don't have anything in common with them, other than the fact that we all have the same blood running through our veins. They can't understand why I'd want to get married—which in their eyes means tied down, and I can't understand why they'd rather go it alone—at least, I didn't understand why until our marriage fell apart," she amended.

She didn't know what she was talking about, he thought angrily. "It *didn't* fall apart," Levi insisted.

"Oh, no?" What universe did this man live in? "Then what would you call this?" she demanded, waving her hand around to indicate the three of them.

Levi responded without hesitation. "A bump in the road."

"A bump?" she repeated, dumbfounded. "This isn't a *bump*, it's a whole mountain range."

He looked at Bekka. She'd drifted to sleep, but was now beginning to stir again. "Lower your voice," he ordered softly. "Before you make her cry again."

Why was *she* always to blame for everything? Especially when the fault was with him. "Maybe it's *you* that's making her cry again."

Taking a breath, he tried once more, even though he could see failure coming from a mile away. "Look, Claire, I'm trying to apologize here." *Again*, he thought with a mounting feeling of hopelessness threatening to cave in on him.

"Apologize?" she asked incredulously. "Is *that* what you're doing? Well, trust me, you're doing a really terrible job of it. As a matter of fact, this is probably the worst apology in history," Claire informed him haughtily.

With that, she turned on her heel and marched back into the boarding house. She didn't stop walking until she got to their room.

Still holding Bekka in her arms, she locked the door to ensure that Levi couldn't get in. Then she put Bekka down in her crib. Her grandfather had gotten it down from the attic when she'd arrived, announcing that she'd left Levi and was staying with them. She drew some comfort from the fact that, according to her grandmother, the crib had once been her father's. It gave her a sense of continuity.

Once Bekka was lying safely in her crib, Claire threw herself facedown on the bedspread and sobbed her heart out.

She hated this. Hated fighting with the only man she now knew she had ever really loved. Most of all, she hated thinking that there was no saving her marriage.

There had to be. But what if Levi decided that she wasn't worth his changing? What if he had been staying away from her on purpose? Using any excuse he could come up with?.

Her tears flowed faster. And her heart ached more.

"I see it's not going as well as you'd like," Gene Strickland commented as he came up behind his grandson-in-law.

The older man had been privy to the latter half of the

exchange between his granddaughter and Levi, taking care to stay out of sight until it was finally over.

He had a feeling that one of them would need a shoulder to cry on—or at least a sounding board.

He wasn't entirely wrong.

Levi turned around to face the older man. "The way I'd like?" he repeated. "Sir, it's not going well in any manner, shape or form," Levi lamented, trying very hard not to allow despair to swallow him up whole.

"Strickland women are not the easiest people to live with at times," Gene agreed sagely. "They can be stubborn and pigheaded," he admitted. "But they can also be loyal and loving. Just don't give up, boy," Claire's grandfather counseled.

"Oh, I have no intentions of giving up," Levi told the man. "But I'm afraid the problem is that Claire doesn't think I'm good enough for her."

If he knew his granddaughter, the reverse was probably true. She probably worried that Levi thought he was too good for her. The family loyalty he'd mentioned kept him from saying that.

Instead, Gene asked, "Where did you get a fool notion like that?"

The origin of his insecurity in this case wasn't hard to trace. "Well, her parents had their doubts about me because I didn't have a college degree like she has."

"A college degree," Gene repeated, scoffing. "That's just a pretty piece of paper. It's what's in here—" he poked a thick finger in the middle of Levi's chest "—that counts, not some piece of paper with fancy lettering. Give me a man who's graduated from the school of hard knocks instead of one who's graduated from some snobbish 'institution of higher learning' any day. Besides, Claire's folks like you. If they knew what was going on, they'd be right here in your corner, egging you on. Telling her to come to her senses."

Levi looked at the man, stunned. He thought the whole town knew about their situation. Strangers were stopping him in the street to share their advice.

"Wait. Her parents don't know?" Gene shook his head in response. "That makes them practically the only ones who don't know," Levi said. "It feels like everyone in town knows and has an opinion about whether or not Claire and I should get back together. God knows I've heard enough of them."

Gene shrugged his wide, squat shoulders. "It's a small town," Gene told him. "Not much happens here by way of entertainment. Folks get bored. I've seen them make bets on how much snow's gonna fall on the first foot of the front step in front of the general store in a given amount of time."

The word *bets* caught Levi's attention. "Are they making bets on my marriage?"

"Wouldn't surprise me," Gene confessed. And then he waved his hand at the whole enterprise. "Don't pay them no mind," he advised. "What counts is how you and Claire-bear feel about your marriage."

Levi turned the nickname over in his mind. Claire-bear. Right now she seemed to be more "bear" than "Claire."

"How do I get her back, Mr. Strickland?" Levi asked unabashedly.

"Patience," Gene said. "And the name's Gene," he told Levi, offering him a friendly grin. "My advice is just be the best you that you can be and always make her feel loved. That's important to a woman," Gene emphasized.

"What if that's not enough?"

"It will be," Gene promised. "That girl was always falling in and out of love when she went to college," he recalled.

Was that supposed to make him feel better? "Then I'm doomed," Levi lamented.

"No, you're not," Gene contradicted. "Like I said, she was always falling in and out of love, but that summer when she came by and told us about you, she lit up like a Christmas tree. I swear there were stars in her eyes. I knew there and then that you had to be the one—and you were."

He sure didn't feel like *the one* right now—unless it meant "the one who got dumped."

"I don't know about that, Mr. Strickland," Levi said quietly, then amended, "I mean, Gene," when the man looked at him expectantly.

"You ever hear that story about the race between the rabbit and the turtle, boy?" Gene asked sagely.

Who hadn't? "Yes, sir," Levi replied respectfully.

"Then you know that that cocky rabbit was all flashy and confident, telling the turtle he was wasting his time competing and should just pull out and quit right at the start. But that turtle didn't pay any attention to that blowhard rabbit. He just kept doing what he was doing, making his way to the finish line by putting one foot in front of the other and damn, if he didn't make it to the finish line before the rabbit, who was busy taking bows and losing sight of the prize. Be that turtle, boy," he said, daring him to be otherwise. "Don't give up until you cross that finish line. In the meantime, I've got more things I need brought up from the basement. You up for it?" he wanted to know, looking at the young man.

In his opinion, it was the very least he could do for the older man after the latter seemed to have taken a shine to him this way. "Yes, sir."

Gene clapped his hand on his grandson-in-law's back. "That's my boy."

At least her grandfather was on his side, Levi thought. Now if he could only get Claire to feel the same way…

Claire took her meal in her room that night, afraid that if she left it, she would immediately run into Levi, and she just didn't feel as if she was up to that.

The truth of it was, her resolve felt rather shaken, and she was afraid that she would just give up and go back with him. The past four weeks would have all been for nothing.

And everyone would think she had no backbone. She *had* to leave Levi—whether or not, deep down, she really wanted to.

Even her grandmother was giving her her space,

Claire thought, not altogether sure she was happy about that turn of events. What if the woman had just given up on her instead? Then what would she do?

As it turned out, Melba gave her until the following morning to deal with whatever feelings she needed to deal with, then let herself in with her pass key.

Walking in, as big as day, she took Claire completely by surprise.

"You scared me, Grandmother," Claire cried, one hand covering the heart that had almost leaped out of her chest.

"I'm not that bad-looking yet," Melba said, disgruntled.

"I didn't mean that," Claire told her, quick to correct any misunderstanding. "I thought you were Levi."

"Levi's gone," Melba said flatly.

The news completely stunned her. "Gone? You mean he's given up?" The thought that he had devastated her. Didn't he care at all? One try and that was it?

"Why?" Melba asked, peering at her closely. "Would you be upset if he had?" Checking the baby's diaper, she made a quick decision and began to change Bekka right then and there.

"Yes. No," Claire amended quickly. "I just thought that since he was here, he'd try harder. Guess he didn't think I was worth it."

"Don't know what he thought," Melba answered crisply. "Don't have the gift that way," her grandmother told her. "Just know that he had to go to work."

"Work? You mean he left for *work*? Does that mean

he's planning on coming back?" Even she heard the hopeful note in her own voice.

"If he's not, he's gonna run out of clothes pretty quick because his suitcase is still in his room," Melba said matter-of-factly, tossing out the dirty diaper.

"Oh." With the immediate threat over, Claire went back to her ambivalent, confused state.

"What that means is that you can come out of hiding," Melba told her, picking the baby up and cradling her in her arms.

"I wasn't hiding," Claire protested.

"Listen to her, Bekka," Melba said to the baby. "She wasn't *hiding*," Melba repeated the word in an animated voice. "Sure she was, wasn't she?" Melba looked up at her granddaughter, her eyes narrowing. "You've got makeup on, don't you?"

"Yes."

It was only eight in the morning. "You sleep in that stuff?"

"No, of course not," she lied, knowing what her grandmother would say if the woman knew that she actually did wear make up to bed so that Levi would always think she looked pretty. It had gotten to be a habit for her. She just continued doing it automatically. "I put it on this morning," she said.

Melba looked her over with a critical eye. "Who are you getting all dolled up for if you're avoiding that lovesick husband of yours?"

"Nobody," Claire lied. "You really think he's lovesick?"

Melba nodded her head. "Worst case I've ever seen."

But Claire pursed her lips together as she shook her head. "I think you're wrong."

Very thin shoulders rose and fell in quick, dismissive succession. "It's a free country. You can think whatever you want to think, even if you're wrong." And it was obvious that she believed that her granddaughter was wrong.

"If he was so lovesick, then why did he stay after the reception and play poker with his friends instead of coming home to me?" Claire challenged.

Melba frowned, unwilling to go another round with this scenario. "You think on that, honey. When you come up with the answer, you'll be ready to be a real wife. Now let's go. We're going to get you fed and then we're going to put you to work. Aren't we, angel?" she asked Bekka.

Bekka cooed in response.

"Good answer," Melba murmured.

Claire sincerely hoped so.

Chapter Six

Claire looked around at her surroundings, more than a little puzzled when her grandmother had stopped walking and turned around to face her.

"This is the kitchen," Claire said in a quizzical tone of voice.

This didn't make any sense. She'd already had her breakfast in the dining room. Why had her grandmother brought her here?

Melba laughed shortly. "Very good. What was your first clue?"

In the past month she had grown rather accustomed to her grandmother's sarcastic retorts. Claire scarcely took note of the older woman's flippant question. But there was something that she knew did need to be asked.

"I thought you said that after breakfast, you were

going to find some work for me to do." She did want to be able to pull her own weight—and to prove to her grandmother that she was a responsible adult rather than just an overgrown child.

"I did and I am," Melba answered crisply. Taking Bekka from her granddaughter, she told the baby—in a far sweeter, softer voice—"You, peanut, are going to keep your great-grandfather company and out of trouble while I put your mama here to work."

Starting to leave, Melba paused to look over her shoulder at Claire. "Stay here," she ordered. "I'll be right back. Talk to Gina while I'm gone," she suggested, waving a hand toward the cook.

Her voice softened just a touch again as she walked out of the kitchen, talking to the baby as if Bekka understood and was hanging on every word.

Feeling a little awkward, Claire looked around the kitchen and offered a quick, small smile to Gina. The latter short, squat, energetic woman was standing by the industrial sink, washing all the dishes, glasses and cutlery that had just been put to use during breakfast. Because there was nothing else for her to do, Claire picked up a towel and began drying everything that Gina had just washed.

The sound of running water and the clanging of dishes was still not enough to really do away with the silence hovering in the room, so Claire tried making polite conversation with the other woman.

"Have you been working for my grandmother long?" She realized only after the words were out of her mouth that she had failed to include her grandfather in that question. But that was because of the two, it was her grandmother who was the more dynamic of the duo and the one who was always very quick to act. That, consequentially, made the woman stand out. Of the two, her grandfather was the slow and steady one, the one who was always dependable, while her grandmother was the bolt of lightning that lit up the sky and just as easily scrambled the brains of anyone who had the misfortune of getting in that lightning bolt's way.

"About two months, now," Gina answered, raising her voice in order to be heard above the clatter. Working with pots now, the noise grew louder, erasing the need for small talk.

But now that she had started, Claire just continued talking. "She can be a little tough," she conceded, wondering if the other woman was holding back because she was afraid she'd lose her job if she complained about her grandmother's bombastic personality.

Gina looked at her over her shoulder. She appeared to be weighing her words before she said, "She's a lady who knows her mind and knows what she wants."

In Claire's estimation, the vague description could easily cover a multitude of sins and transgressions. Gina was apparently being diplomatic.

Claire nodded her head. "And isn't afraid to go get it," she added.

"Being afraid is a waste of time," Melba said, coming up behind the two younger women.

Startled, Claire jumped. She hadn't expected her

grandmother to be back so soon. For a heavyset woman, she moved rather noiselessly. Claire flashed her a spasmodic smile that vanished as quickly as it had appeared. "I guess you found Grandpa right away."

"No, I left Bekka in the living rooom in the potted plant stand." Her grandmother said the words so calmly, for one terrible second, Claire actually thought that the woman was being serious.

And then she realized her grandmother was merely being sarcastic. "Oh, you're kidding. Wow." Claire blew out a breath, attempting to steady her nerves. "For a second you had me really going there."

Melba paused to stare at her granddaughter, and then she shook her head.

"What goes through that head of yours, girl?" she wanted to know. But the very next moment the woman held up her hand like a police officer directing traffic, except that instead of the flow of cars, her grandmother's intention was to hold back any flow of words that might be coming her way. "No, never mind. Don't tell me. I'd rather not know. If I don't know, it won't depress me. Just in case you're unclear about your daughter's whereabouts, Bekka is with your grandfather. Whatever other faults he might have, your grandfather is an excellent babysitter.

"Now, after you finish helping Gina with the rest of kitchen cleanup, she is going to teach you some of the very basics so that you can start helping her prepare the meals here."

Claire stared at her grandmother, stunned. They'd already had this conversation weeks ago. "Grandmother, I can't cook," she protested with feeling. " We eat a lot of…frozen food," she said lamely, knowing what her grandmother was likely to say about *that*!

About to leave the kitchen, Melba turned and fixed her with a look that seemed to penetrate straight into her bones.

"Can't or won't?" Melba challenged.

"Can't," Claire answered in a very small, helpless voice.

It was obvious by her grandmother's expression that the woman thought otherwise. "When you lose a limb, you *can't* grow it back. It's not possible. That is *not* the case when it comes to cooking. Just because you're currently burning water when you boil it doesn't mean that you're doomed to keep repeating that mistake. You *can* learn how to cook and you *will* learn how to cook," she instructed. "You just need to have someone who is good at it teach you what to do. Gina here," Melba said, gesturing toward the other woman, "is the very best."

Gina smiled, somewhat dazed at the compliment. Everyone knew that it wasn't often that the woman had anything positive to say. This was a very rare moment.

"Thank you, Mrs. Strickland. But I'm not really very good at teaching someone," Gina politely protested.

Melba turned to look at the cook. She had just one word for her.

"Learn."

And with that, Melba left the kitchen. Her very bearing indicated that she expected any miracles that needed to be called into play to be done so, efficiently and quickly.

Gina looked far from happy about the situation, but at the same time she appeared to be stoically resigned to her fate.

"Did you really burn water?" Gina asked her new apprentice.

Claire flushed and stared down at her shoes as she nodded her answer. She took no pride in the fact that the answer to the question was affirmative. She silently nodded her head, thinking that there were really a couple of excuses—one weaker than the next—to be said in her defense.

No one had ever gone out of their way in any manner to attempt to teach her how to cook when she was growing up. Coupled with that was that she had never had the slightest desire to learn. When she was growing up, there was always someone to do the cooking. She ate without giving the meal's preparation a second thought.

When she was finally on her own, away at college, she subsisted on take-out foods and the occasional microwave specials that required from ninety seconds to six minutes of microwave time, no more. The meals were basically satisfactory with no fuss involved.

When she first married Levi, she'd made a couple of halfhearted attempts at cooking before returning to her tried-and-true avenues of provisions: takeouts and microwaveable meals.

Occasionally, Levi would cook or they would go out. Or at least they had gone out before Bekka was born.

Having the baby around changed almost everything, including her eating habits.

Especially when Levi was away on business.

Without giving it much thought, Claire subsisted on sandwiches and microwavable meals.

"So, what *do* you know how to cook?" Gina asked her once the last pot had been washed, dried and put away some twenty minutes later. Her tone of voice indicated that she really didn't believe that the girl standing next to her wasn't able to cook *anything*.

Claire took a deep breath before answering. She did her best not to feel inadequate. "Nothing," she answered honestly.

"O-kay," Gina said, taking the response in stride. It was clear that she was looking for something positive to be gleaned from this. "That means there's nothing to unlearn. Good. We'll start out with a clean slate."

Claire waited a beat longer, holding her breath. Expecting something more derogatory to be said in reference to her lack of any basic culinary skills.

When nothing followed, she released a long sigh of relief. She'd thought that Gina would say something belittling or snide about the fact that she had reached her present age of twenty-four without learning how to even scramble an egg properly—hers came out looking as if they'd been uncovered in a war zone.

A *major* war zone, Claire thought ruefully, remembering her last effort.

"Okay, so this is what we're going to do. We're going to start with the very basics and build up from there,"

Gina told her, giving the impression of mentally rolling up her sleeves. "Do you know how to make mashed potatoes?"

Claire pressed her lips together. She was well aware that she had to be coming across like some sort of an inept idiot. But she didn't know enough to bluff her way through this. She was forced to own up to the truth.

"No," she admitted.

"After today, you will," Gina told her so matter-of-factly that Claire found herself believing the older woman.

It wasn't easy, and he was tired enough to briefly consider just going back to his apartment right here in Bozeman and crashing there after the day he had put in at the store.

A day that required double duty from him in order to be able to leave the store at something approaching regular hours.

But the apartment was as hauntingly empty as ever. He couldn't endure that. It was almost like living with ghosts. After all, they'd had some happy times living in the apartment before things began to go bad.

So, even though he had to push himself, Levi made his mind up and was driving back to Rust Creek Falls. He was doing it in order to at least be sleeping under the same general roof as Claire and the baby.

One baby step at a time in order to get back to where he once was, he told himself.

With one eye watching for any telltale signs of patrol

cars hiding in the shadows, hoping to hand out speeding tickets, Levi wound up making remarkably good time with no mishaps.

Parking his vehicle in the first place he could, he hurried into the boarding house and toward the stairs. He was hoping to be able to at least take one peek into Claire's room to catch a glimpse of her and the baby.

If she let him.

But before he could even reach the staircase, Gene saw him and called him over into the sitting room. The second Levi started to approach, he saw that the older man was not alone.

Levi cut the distance between them quickly.

"Thought you might want to say hi to your best girl here," Gene told him. "Or at least one of them." The man amended his own statement with a wink. Lowering his face so it was next to the baby's, Gene coaxed, "Bekka, say hi to your daddy."

Drained though he was, Levi all but melted at the sight of his daughter. To him she was a ray of sunshine in a disposable diaper. His heart was instantly warm and overflowing with love.

"How's the most beautiful eight-month-old girl in the whole wide world?" Levi asked Bekka.

He picked his daughter up from the very frilly bassinet she was lying in. Gene had gone out and bought the bassinet for her the very first time Claire had brought the baby by for a visit. He'd said he thought it was a very worthwhile investment, even though Bekka would be quick to outgrow it.

"You can always save it for the next baby," Gene had told Claire. He'd had a hopeful gleam in his eye at the time.

In Levi's overjoyed estimation, his daughter looked as if she was excited to see him. Bekka began to wave her tiny fists around while she started to gurgle and coo. A series of tiny, interconnected bubbles were cascading from her lips, formed out of the formula that she'd had earlier.

The resulting mess didn't bother Levi in the slightest. In all honesty, the entire sight pleased him no end.

Taking out his handkerchief, he wiped the drool marks from his daughter's mouth and chin.

"I see your great-grandpa's keeping you fed," he told the baby with a pleased laugh. Mission accomplished, he shoved his handkerchief back into his pocket. "Did you miss your daddy?" He asked the baby the question as seriously as if he was addressing a ten-year-old. "I hate leaving you, baby, but Daddy has to go to work so that you can have all the formula that you want."

Picking Bekka up and holding her close, Levi heard his daughter continue to make a few more noises.

One noise in particular had him suddenly freezing in place.

His lower jaw dropped.

Stunned, he immediately turned toward Gene to see if the other man had heard it, as well, or if his imagination and overwrought state were just playing tricks on him.

"Did you hear that?" he asked in what amounted to

a hushed whisper, afraid that if he voiced the question any louder, the moment would be gone.

"I did, indeed," Gene confirmed, beaming because he was thoroughly pleased with this turn of events. He had always liked his granddaughter's choice of a partner for all eternity.

"She said 'Da,'" Levi cried, utterly thrilled beyond words. And then his eyes shifted back to Gene, his witness in this joyous matter. "She did say 'Da,' right? I mean, you heard her say it. It's not just me, is it?"

Levi's state of ecstasy tickled the older man. He identified with it completely. There was just nothing to compare to the moment that a child suddenly chooses to identify you and bond with that identification. He remembered how it had been with his own boys.

"No, it's not just you and yes, I heard her say it," Gene told him with a laugh.

Another thought suddenly hit Levi. "Is that normal?" he wanted to know. "I mean, do babies her age actually talk?"

Maybe she was some sort of a prodigy, he thought, his mind already racing and making half-formed plans.

"Not so's you can carry on an actual conversation," Gene told him, "but some babies have been known to say a word or two. Or at least make sounds that *sounded* like words." Gene ran his hand lightly over the back of Bekka's exceptionally soft hair. "And this little princess here did say 'Da.' We both heard her. It's a red-letter day. Bekka said her first word."

The moment the impact of the older man's last sentence sank in, the extremely wide grin on Levi's lips faded a degree, replaced by a look of concern. "You can't tell Claire." It was both an instruction and a plea on Levi's part.

Gene didn't quite understand why that was so important to Bekka's dad. "Because you want to be the first one to tell her?" he guessed.

Levi shook his head. "No, no, I don't want to tell her. I don't want *anyone* to tell her. I don't want Claire to know," he insisted.

Gene's shaggy eyebrows drew together over his brow like two hairy spiders. "I don't think I understand."

"When we were still living together in the apartment, Claire spent a lot of her time with the baby while I was working. Her whole life was centered around feeding Bekka, changing Bekka, bathing Bekka—you get the picture," he said, halting the barrage of examples. "For Claire it was almost nothing but Bekka 24/7. After putting in all that time with the baby, to have Bekka's first word be 'Da' instead of 'Mama,' well, it'll just devastate her."

That Levi was so concerned about Claire's feelings was nothing short of touching, Gene thought. "Maybe you're underestimating her."

But Levi apparently didn't think so. "Claire's got feelings, and those feelings can get really hurt," Levi told the older man. "I don't want to take a chance that I'm actually right about this."

"What if Bekka says it in front of Claire? That could happen," Gene pointed out.

"We'll have to take our chances. Maybe she'll say 'Mama,'" Levi said hopefully.

Based on his own children, Gene had his doubts about that. "So you really don't want me to tell her?" Gene questioned. After all, a baby's first word was a really big deal for her parents.

"No," Levi answered. "It's just better if Claire doesn't know."

"What's better if Claire doesn't know?" Claire asked, picking that moment to walk into the room. She had put in close to five hours in the kitchen under Gina's tutelage, and she was utterly exhausted.

But on the outside chance that she might just bump into Levi tonight, she'd hurried to her room to freshen up her makeup and comb her hair into some sort of an attractive style—just in case. She didn't want Levi to *ever* see her looking anything but perfect. She was afraid that he would be disappointed if that ever happened. Her wobbly self-esteem couldn't handle the blow.

Claire looked expectantly now from one man to the other, waiting for an answer.

"I thought it was better if you didn't know that I broke a couple of speed limits getting here from work," Levi told her, improvising on the spot. "I didn't get a ticket, but just the same, I didn't want you getting mad that I broke the law. I guess I was really anxious to get back to you and the baby," he repeated, giving her the most soulful look he could.

"Well, you shouldn't do that," Claire told him. "Speeding tickets are expensive." Then a hint of a smile broke through and she added almost shyly, "But I do understand why you did it."

And it secretly did please her very, very much.

Chapter Seven

Maybe she'd been too hasty, throwing Levi out of their apartment—and her life—the way she had, Claire thought a few days later. She was walking through the quaint streets of Rust Creek Falls, pushing Bekka in the carriage that she and Levi had picked out together a week before Bekka was born.

She remembered the day clearly because she had literally *begged* Levi to let her get out of bed for what had amounted to a rare outing. The latter half of her pregnancy had been exceedingly difficult for her, and the doctor had recommended complete bed rest just to remain on the safe side.

At first, surrounded with books and all the things she'd wanted to catch up on, bed rest had almost been welcomed. It was certainly no big hardship. However, after three months of looking at the same four walls, day in, day out, Claire felt as if she was in danger of going completely crazy.

Since she'd been feeling stronger and by her own assessment, hadn't been feeling violently ill in a long while, she had begged and pleaded with Levi to take her outside of their apartment.

To take her *anywhere* as long as it didn't involve those same four walls.

Eventually, Levi had reluctantly given in and agreed. But rather than allow her to walk outside, her chivalrous cowboy husband had carried her into their flatbed truck. Since he was trying to cheer her up, Levi hinted that he had a specific destination in mind. She'd badgered him, but he had remained steadfast and secretive until they finally got there.

He'd driven them over to a store that dealt exclusively in baby items, from furnishings to clothes to toys. The owner, a friendly man named Jamie Pierce, turned out to be someone Levi had met and struck up a friendship with at one of those seminars he had been required to attend. The upshot of that was that they got a really good deal on the baby carriage.

What she remembered from that day was not the deal, but the fact that Levi had carried her to and from the truck, and that he had surprised her with the baby carriage, one she had seen in a catalog and had wistfully been pining after for the past few months.

The carriage had come unassembled. Levi brought the box into their bedroom so that she could witness the process and offer her suggestions from the sidelines while he stayed up half the night putting all the carriage pieces together. She'd fallen asleep watching him. All she knew was that in the morning, when she woke up, the carriage had been assembled and Levi had already left for work. A simple calculation told her that he had gone to work on—at most—approximately three hours' sleep.

It struck her as truly selfless.

He was a good father, Claire thought now as she crossed the street. And not exactly that shabby a husband, either. Not everyone would have gone out of their way like that to indulge a frustrated, housebound pregnant wife.

What had she been thinking?

The answer was she hadn't been thinking. She'd been too quick to allow her emotions to dictate her actions, she told herself. Before acting on a whim like that, she should have counted to ten—and then ten more. Hardworking, loving men like Levi were hard to find. Tossing him aside like that was crazy.

She just hadn't been herself that July Fourth weekend.

Chewing on her bottom lip, she looked down at Bekka. The baby was still asleep, lulled by the soothing feel of the summer sun warming the area around her, if not her directly.

It was time to start heading back.

But unintentionally, she had just crossed the collective path of a group of Rust Creek Falls' senior citizens, otherwise regarded by some as the town's opinionated, unofficial Greek chorus. They behaved as if they were qualified—and actually obligated—to express their opinions on everything that transpired in the small town.

Today was no exception.

"Heard you gave that no-show husband of yours his walking papers, dearie," Blanche Curtis, an older woman sitting on the extreme left of the bench in front of the One-Stop General Store said to her. The woman had gray hair, more than her share of wrinkles thanks to an unforgiving sun and looked as if she would be perfectly at home playing the wicked witch in a revival of *The Wizard of Oz*. "Good for you," she cried encouragingly. "That'll teach him to take you for granted.

"These men," she continued, casting a critical eye toward her seatmates on the other end of the bench. "They tell you that you're the moon and the stars to them, then they get you pregnant and pretty quick, they lose all interest in you. 'Time to move on to new challenges,'" Blanche said in disgust, shaking her head. "They're all about the hunt and conquest, nothing else."

"I'm sorry," Claire said, unable to get away because the woman was holding on to the side of the carriage with her long, thin fingers, "do I know you?"

"No, but I know you," the woman told her with an air of mystery. "Blanche Curtis," the woman told her, sticking out her hand. "I'm a friend of your grandma's," she added, as if that explained everything.

"If you're such a great friend, why are you trying to

mess with her granddaughter's life and give her advice she doesn't need?" the man sitting on the far side of the bench wanted to know.

"I beg your pardon." Blanche sniffed indignantly. The woman sat up a little straighter, as if that could help her repel any unwanted criticism from the man on the end.

"Don't beg for my pardon, beg for hers," the man said, nodding his head toward Claire. Leaning both hands on the ornate head of his sleek, black cane, he slid forward on the seat just a tad. "Don't pay her any mind, Claire. She's been a bitter old woman since the third grade when Michael Finnegan picked Rachel White to be his square-dance partner instead of her. You put that family of yours together the first chance you get, young lady," the man advised. "A baby deserves to have both a mama and a daddy."

"Billy Joe Ryan, you do an awful lot of talking for a man with no brain," the woman who had introduced herself as Blanche angrily accused.

"Now, Blanche, leave the poor girl alone," a third member of the unofficial town philosophers' group, Homer Gilmore, said. "Can't you see that she's thinking about doing the right thing? Everyone deserves a second chance, even a husband," he said with enthusiastic conviction. And then he turned toward Claire. "You give that man of yours a second chance, Miss Claire," he advised nervously. "You'll be happy you did. You don't like being alone, right?"

Claire stared at the man who she vaguely remembered meeting once before, at the wedding reception. He seemed to be very convinced that she needed to forgive Levi. Why would it matter to him one way or another?

Didn't these people have anything better to do than to sit around, giving out unwanted advice?

"Better alone than being with a man who doesn't care just how much he hurts his wife with his actions," the fourth member on the bench, a woman she'd heard referred to as "Alice" at the reception, proclaimed.

Claire could only take in this unwanted commentary on her life in abject horror. Did *everyone* in this town have an opinion on her marital state and on whether or not she should take Levi back?

The very thought unnerved her and made her want to run for cover. Didn't these people have *lives* of their own?

Upset and protective of her family's right to privacy, Claire asked, "Is that all you people talk about? The state of my marriage?"

"Lately, it's been pretty much of an equal draw between your marriage and the weather," she heard a deep voice behind her saying.

Claire whirled around, startled. Her attention focused on the four people who had just rendered very public their opinions about the very private matter of her home life, Claire hadn't been aware of anyone coming up behind her until just now when he spoke.

When she'd swung around, she was still holding on to the handle of the baby carriage and brought it abruptly around with her. The result was that she came within a hair's breadth of whacking a man's legs with the carriage.

Sucking in her breath, she pulled the carriage to her and away from the man.

"I'm so sorry," Claire apologized then added in her own defense, "but you snuck up on me."

"Wasn't planning it that way. I'm Detective Russ Campbell," he told her. Even as he spoke, all four occupants of the bench seemed to lean forward in unison, obviously intent on hearing what was being said. Campbell was just as intent that they didn't. "Listen, is there anywhere that you and I could go to have a few words?" He left the choice up to her. "I'd like to ask you some questions."

What possible reason would an officer of the law have to question her? Claire couldn't help wondering. Was this because of something that Levi had done, because, to the very best of her knowledge, she certainly wasn't guilty of anything.

Except for cooking, maybe, she silently amended.

"What kind of questions?" Claire wanted to know. Out of the corner of her eye, she saw that the four people on the bench seemed to have moved closer to the side where she and the officer were standing.

"The kind you wouldn't want the people around here to speculate about," Russ wisely replied.

Claire lowered her voice. "You mean it could get worse than this?" she asked incredulously.

The detective laughed at the naive question. "Can it

ever," he said to her. "I believe the old expression that best summarizes this is, 'You ain't seen nothin' yet.'"

That was all she needed, Claire thought, to have the whole town talking and speculating about something in her life.

As if she didn't have enough to deal with.

"Okay, you talked me into it," she told him. And then she remembered. She had obligations now. She didn't want to give her grandmother any reason to think she was behaving irresponsibly. It was a matter of pride. "But will this take long? I have to be getting back to help out with lunch. I'm staying at the Strickland Boarding House," she added.

An easy smile curved the cop's lips. "Yes, I know. I was just getting ready to go over there to see you."

This was beginning to come together for her. "Oh, so I didn't just bump into you."

"Not exactly," he told her.

Claire turned her back to the bench and its occupants, not wanting to give the foursome an opportunity to eavesdrop. "You could come back there with me," she suggested. "We could talk on the way."

Russ glanced over his shoulder and saw four pairs of eyes watching them intently. However, he seemed fairly certain that none of the four would be willing to rise and follow behind them for the sake of satisfying any latent curiosity.

Russ nodded. "Sounds good to me."

Without bothering to say goodbye or anything else to

the foursome, Claire started walking back to the boarding house, pushing Bekka's carriage in front of her.

The detective fell into step beside her.

"What is it you want to know?" she asked.

"On the night of the wedding that you and your husband attended, did you notice anything out of the ordinary going on at the reception?"

She certainly hadn't expected the detective to question her about the harmless wedding reception.

"Out of the ordinary?" Claire repeated, confused. Thinking back to that night, she felt that the goings-on at the reception had all been slightly out of the ordinary. The reception was one big party, and parties were all about people cutting loose. Since it wasn't just a wedding reception but also the Fourth of July, that was to be expected—wasn't it?

"Yes." Russ tried rephrasing his question. "Was anyone behaving suspiciously?"

Claire thought for a moment, but nothing really came to mind. "No, I don't think so."

Russ became more specific. "Did you by any chance notice anyone slipping something into people's drinks, or into the punch bowl?"

That was something she would not have just taken notice of, but mentioned to either Levi or later on to her grandfather. But she hadn't observed anything of the kind.

"No, of course not." Did the man actually think she would have taken that in stride? "I would have said something if I'd seen someone doing that." And then she replayed the detective's question in her mind. "Why? Do you think someone was tampering with people's drinks at the reception?" she asked, horrified by the very thought and what it implied.

Russ didn't answer her directly. Instead, he asked her another question. "Think back to that night. Do you think that anyone had a reason to slip a mickey into your drink?"

Claire blinked. "*My* drink? Why would anyone slip something into my drink?" she wanted to know. There was no reason for the officer to think anything like that. She wasn't a threat to anyone. Nor did she have any enemies or even friendly rivals. "I was planning on going home with my husband when the reception was over."

"But you didn't," Russ pointed out.

"No, I didn't." It took effort to say that without a trace of bitterness. "Levi decided he wanted to join in a poker game some of the guys were getting up."

"Was that usual behavior for him?" Russ asked.

"Usual?" she echoed, not sure what the cop was asking.

Russ rephrased the question. "Does he go off to play poker a lot?"

"No, as a matter of fact, he's *never* done that." *See, even you have to admit that it was unusual for Levi to walk off and leave you like that. Something's just not right here.* "Do you think that someone slipped him something?"

"Do *you* think that?" Russ asked, turning the question back around on her.

"I don't know," she said helplessly. "Levi seemed normal enough. I mean, he wasn't slurring or weaving or anything like that." She got back to the officer's question. "What reason would anyone have to spike his drink?" Claire asked.

Russ tried to make himself clearer. He was still trying to clarify the situation for himself. "I don't think he was targeted specifically. I think that a lot of people might have been affected by the punch being spiked."

"So the punch *was* spiked?" she repeated incredulously. "But why would anyone want to do that?" Claire wanted to know.

That was the giant knot he was attempting to untangle. "That's what I'm trying to find out," Russ told her. "Did anything strike you as being odd that evening?" he asked again. "Anything overall?"

Claire pressed her lips together, thinking. "Well, now that you mention it...*I* felt kind of odd that evening. I mean, I'm small and it doesn't take much to make me feel light-headed, but even I can hold down one drink, or even two, without having the room go spinning around."

Russ stopped walking and looked at her. "And did it?" he asked her. "The room, did it go spinning around for you?"

"Yes," she admitted, recalling the unpleasant sensation. "It did. What does that mean?" she asked him. "I mean, aside from the fact that someone might have tampered with the punch. Why would someone do that? What was there to gain?"

The officer shook his head. "I don't really know. Yet," Russ added. "But I will," he promised. "I will."

Claire couldn't wait for Levi to come back to the boarding house that evening. All through her chores, as she assisted Gina with both lunch and the evening meal, her mind kept going back to the fateful night of the wedding reception.

But nothing enlightening came to her.

The officer had told her that he suspected someone had tampered with the punch, causing everyone who drank it to behave erratically.

But she hadn't.

And Levi hadn't.

Levi hadn't behaved erratically at all. He had just tuned her out and gone off with his friends. That was behaving thoughtlessly, she told herself, not erratically.

Right?

Stop giving the man excuses.

But what if that *had* been Levi's excuse? What if Levi's drink *had* been spiked? That meant that he hadn't been himself that night and couldn't be held accountable for just leaving her like that to go play cards with his friends.

Okay, that was *that* night, but what about all the other nights? The nights that he was out late "working" or away altogether, in another town, at some so-called "furniture" seminar—whatever *that* was.

And what if it hadn't been a seminar? What if Levi

was entertaining an out-of-town guest? A party of one, emphasis on the word *party*?

The very thought that he might be cheating on her, that he had gotten tired of her and maybe struck up a "friendship" with some other younger, prettier, *single* woman began to prey on her mind, making her conjure up a host of terrible scenarios.

By the time Levi returned to the boarding house that evening, it was rather late. Even so, he made it a point to stop at Claire's room and knock on her door. When she didn't answer, he tried again.

There was still no answer.

He knew she wasn't downstairs in the common room because he'd checked there first before coming up.

Had she gone back home? If not that, then what? He'd thought that they were making progress, taking baby steps, but still making progress. But maybe he was wrong.

A feeling of desperation began to mount up within him as he knocked yet a third time. If she didn't answer this time, he was going to go look for her grandfather and—

The door opened. Relief flooded through him, but it was short-lived.

Claire was holding the door ajar, placing her own body in the way like a human doorstop. Levi couldn't get in unless he pushed her out of the way, which he wasn't about to do.

"Detective Campbell wants to talk to you," she told

him coolly. Her body language made it crystal clear that he wasn't setting foot into the room.

"Detective Campbell?" he questioned, trying to put the name to a face. He failed. "About what?"

Claire drew herself up to her full height. "About the night of the reception."

That still really didn't answer his question. "What about it?" he wanted to know.

Claire's eyes met his. "He wants to know if you think you were drugged at the time."

"Drugged? You mean he thinks I took drugs?" Claire wasn't being very clear about this, he thought. "You know I don't do that kind of thing," he told her.

When she didn't immediately respond, telling him that she knew he would never take any sort of unlawful substance, that he was far too responsible to do something like that, Levi was quick to swear an oath. "May I never see my little girl again if I took so much as a larger dosage of aspirin, much less some kind of an illegal drug."

She regarded him for a very long moment, as if she was weighing several things. In the end, she relented. Sort of.

"I believe that *you* don't think you took any kind of an illegal drug, but maybe someone managed to slip you something without your knowledge." Cocking her head, she peered at him, as if a different angle could somehow give her a better perspective. "Would you even know?"

Having had absolutely no experience with any of

that, he shrugged. "I guess that depends on what it was and what the dosage was."

"But offhand? What did you feel that night, after the wedding reception?" Claire pressed, wanting to see what he would say to her.

He thought about it for a long moment, trying to re-create the time frame in his mind. "Maybe I felt a little hyper and somewhat wired." That sounded so lame, he thought, but that was the best he could describe it. "All I know was that I was looking forward to playing poker."

Her eyes narrowed slightly. Well, now she knew. "But not to being with me."

Damn, she was doing it again, Levi thought. She was putting words into his mouth. "I never said that," he protested.

"You didn't have to," she informed him, her hurt galvanizing her again. "Good night!" she cried. Pushing him back, she slammed the door right in his face.

Chapter Eight

She was doing it again, Levi thought glumly. Claire was shutting him out.

He thought that they were finally making progress, and now Claire was giving him the cold shoulder every time they were within a couple feet of each other.

To his overwhelming dismay, this had been going on for a couple of days now, and he was pretty much at his wit's end as to how to win her back or even how to wear her down so that they were back to where they'd been just a few days ago.

He had thought that whatever set Claire off the other evening would have faded away by now. That they would be back to that cautious two-step they were doing, dancing around the issues and the sensitive feelings that were involved while trying to slowly work their way back to where they'd been before this whole wedding reception/Fourth of July fiasco had ever happened.

But they weren't. At least, Claire wasn't.

As for him, he was more than willing to go down on bended knee to ask her forgiveness if that was what it took. He just wanted to get Claire past this hurdle and back on track. Back to being his wife and the mother of his beloved baby girl.

It was getting worse, not better. He missed being with Claire and the baby like crazy. Missed the silent comfort of their ordinary, day-to-day lives.

But each time they'd cross paths, Claire would deliberately and pointedly look away, as if looking at him caused her more distress and annoyance than she could bear.

There had to be something he could do to change that. But what?

The thought that he couldn't think of anything really bothered him as Levi stood near the front door of the furniture store. Knowing that he had a full day of work ahead of him, he managed to plaster a cheerful, albeit very hollow smile on his face.

It was hard for him to keep his mind on business when everything inside him felt as if it was in complete turmoil.

But he knew he had to continue this charade he was presently engaged in. If he didn't—if he allowed the situation to get the better of him and make him fall apart—he'd wind up putting his job in jeopardy, and that was totally unacceptable.

He couldn't dare risk losing his job. Besides having worked long and hard to get to where he was, working here at the furniture store represented the only source of income that he had. Without any income, he knew he was *sure* to lose Claire and Bekka.

The thought struck him as being ironic, since it was initially his job—and the long hours that it required him to keep—that had torn his little family apart in the first place.

There were presently several customers in the store, wandering through the various artfully arranged furnishings that he had personally staged and set up. Levi kept his distance from the potential clients, instinctively knowing that there was nothing that drove customers away faster than a salesperson who hovered, or worse, one who offered a running commentary on whatever piece they might be looking at.

He'd learned early on that customers appreciated being given their space to view and debate before they came to their final decision. If they needed any assistance of any sort, he knew for a fact that they would seek him out.

All he had to do was wait and make himself available to them.

If he was only certain that the same theory was true when it came to Claire. He swore she was like the proverbial wild card that could pop up in a hand at any time. He had absolutely no idea what she was thinking or what she was liable to do. All he knew with certainty was that he had to win her back. As to when and how, well, that was anyone's guess. He certainly didn't have a clue. All he could do was make himself available.

And pray.

His cell phone rang. Pulling it out of his pocket, he answered the phone before it could ring again.

"So how's it going?" the feminine voice on the other end of the line asked.

For just a moment he found the familiarity of his mother's voice comforting. But he wasn't a little boy anymore, and the days that she could make all things right were long gone.

"It's not, Ma," he said honestly. "It's stalled."

There was a long pause on the other end before his mother told him, "It's only stalled if you want it to be."

He refrained from telling his mother that he was attempting to move heaven and earth—and not getting very far doing it. "It's not that simple, Ma."

"It's also not as complicated as you're making it, Levi," Lucy Wyatt told him. "First of all, you have to give yourself permission to be happy. That doesn't mean working yourself to death," she added pointedly.

His mother, he recalled, always worried that he was working too hard. "I'm not, Ma."

Lucy dismissed her son's words. "Oh, if I know you, you are, Levi. And I blame myself for that. I shouldn't have allowed you to turn your back on furthering your education by going out to work right after high school graduation. I know that you did that strictly to help out your brothers, as well as me.

"You're a good boy, Levi," she went on. "Your motives were pure and noble when you took that job. But mine weren't. I should have known better. I shouldn't have accepted the money that you turned over to me." A deep sadness entered her voice as Lucy said, "I sold out your childhood for a paycheck. What kind of a mother does that make me?"

"You are a great mother, and I was hardly a child, Ma," he pointed out.

He could hear the tightness in her throat as she said, "That's right, you hardly were. And that was my fault. When your father walked out on us, leaving me to raise and provide for the three of you, I let you take those part-time jobs, turning a blind eye to what that would eventually mean. I allowed you to put in all those long hours working while your friends were out having fun, being young. You never got that chance."

He didn't want his mother berating herself for what had been his decision. "They were just being kids, Ma," Levi said dismissively.

"Exactly! Something you should have had a right to be, too," she insisted.

He didn't want her to beat herself up for what he felt was one of the better decisions of his life. "I'll do it the second time around."

"The second time?" Lucy repeated, bewildered. "I don't understand."

He laughed. "They say that when people get very old, they regress to their childhood and start behaving like little kids. I'll get to it then," Levi told his mother. "Don't worry about it."

But it was obvious that she did.

However, since it was also obvious that the conversation wasn't going anywhere with this topic, Lucy Wyatt switched back to the topic that had initially prompted her to call her son in the first place.

"So how's the campaign to win back your touchy wife going?"

"Ma—" There was a hint of a warning note in his voice. He and Claire might be having their problems, and he knew that his mother was on his side no matter what, but he couldn't just stand by and allow blame to be heaped on Claire's head this way.

"Sorry," Lucy apologized with little enthusiasm. However, it was clear that she had no intentions of antagonizing her son, either. "How's the campaign to win back your wife going?" she reworded.

Levi refrained from blowing out a long breath. He didn't want to call any undue attention to himself from any of the people currently in the store. "It's not."

Lucy's voice was filled with tenderness as she made her son this offer. "Honey, would you like me to talk to her for you?"

He felt a chill streaking down his back at the very thought of what she was saying. "God forbid. It'll set Claire off. No offense, Ma, but you're not exactly a disinterested party here."

Lucy had never been anything but honest when dealing with her sons. She respected them too much as human beings to indulge in any verbal games.

"No, I'm not. I'm a *very* interested party. You're a

good person and you deserve the best, Levi. I just get upset when I see you being treated with anything but the utmost love and respect," she confessed.

She was putting him up on a pedestal again, Levi thought. She had to stop doing that and get more realistic. "I'm not perfect, Ma."

"Maybe not, but then neither is she," Lucy said loyally. "And besides, there's a baby's happiness at stake here. Bekka needs you in her life." Emotion throbbed in her voice as she told her son, "I won't have Claire painting you as the bad guy."

"She's not, Ma. Really," he told his mother. "Don't take this the wrong way, but please stay out of it." In a moment of weakness and at a very low point, he'd told his mother about their argument and his subsequent— and hopefully temporary—change of address. He more than regretted it now.

It was obvious that his mother wasn't buying his protests, but being his mother, she also didn't want to argue about it since it clearly upset him.

Lucy cast about for another way to help her oldest son. "Maybe if I got together with Claire's mother and father and talked to them… If I made them see that they really needed to talk some sense into their daughter's head—"

That would just make everything that much worse, Levi thought. Didn't his mother see that? She wouldn't have wanted anyone butting into her private affairs. "Ma, promise me you won't interfere." He was all but begging now.

"All right, as long as you promise me you won't give up trying to talk some sense into that girl. I don't want my granddaughter growing up without her father—or her father's mother," Lucy added.

That makes two of us, Ma, Levi thought. "I promise, and Bekka won't, don't worry."

"But I *do* worry," Lucy told her son. "I'm your mother. It's my job to worry. Now promise you'll call me the minute you two get back together."

"Yes, Ma," Levi replied dutifully. "I promise. Look, I've got to go. I'm at the store and I've got a customer who wants to make a purchase—"

"Look at you, making a sale without saying a word," Lucy commented proudly. "I hope your boss knows what a prize you are."

Levi rolled his eyes. He knew if he let her, his mother could go on like that for hours, and he loved her for it. But not right now.

"He does."

"Maybe *he* can talk to your wife, since I can't," Lucy said with a touch of exasperation in her voice.

He knew he had to quit now while he still could. "Bye, Ma. I'm hanging up now," he told her, and then terminated the call.

Although the store did have customers—and one had even looked his way—no one had approached him, indicating that they were ready to talk business. He'd only said that to his mother to get off the phone. He had the uneasy feeling that not only wasn't his mother going to cease and desist, but she was also most likely going to attempt to broker some sort of mediation between himself and Claire.

There would be no way he would even remotely agree to anything his mother had in mind because he was certain that he would be risking having things become even worse than they were at the present moment.

His mother, unfortunately, had that way about her. Besides, what woman wanted to have her mother-in-law butting in to her life?

All he could do, Levi thought as he quietly observed the customers meandering through the various displays in the store, was to make himself as readily available as he could to Claire and hope for the best.

When he finally came back to the boarding house that night, he was just as wiped out as he had been all the previous nights. The drive back to Rust Creek Falls and the boarding house seemed to get longer every evening. But even though he was having trouble putting one foot in front of the other, he still stopped by Claire's room, hoping against hope she would allow him a glimpse of their daughter.

He had even brought flowers with him to smooth the path.

This time, when he knocked on Claire's door, it opened immediately. That it did caught him completely by surprise, especially since Claire had been turning a deaf ear to his knocking—no matter how hard or how long—on the previous last two nights.

When the door opened Levi unconsciously squeezed

the bouquet he was holding a little harder, but made no effort to offer the flowers to her. In actuality, he'd temporarily forgotten that he was clutching them.

Claire was wearing a tank top that didn't quite cover her midriff, and she had on a pair of denim shorts that brought new meaning to the term *cutoffs*. The whimsical fringes that had resulted from the so-called "cut" barely covered what they were intended to cover, flirting outrageously with the eye of the beholder. In addition, the somewhat faded material clung to her curves as if it had been painted on instead of hastily sewn together in some shop.

Levi had to remind himself to breathe. Periodically. And deeply.

And then he looked more closely at the expression on her face. It didn't look like the kind of expression a woman wearing a sexy tank top and pulse-accelerating shorts would have on her face.

Something was definitely up.

"Your mother called."

The three little words swiftly brought down the world he thought he was about to enter in less than three seconds.

"Oh, God," he groaned, afraid to begin to imagine the damage his mother had caused. "I'm sorry, Claire. I told her I didn't want her getting involved or saying anything to you, but my mother has always been a very headstrong woman."

"Nothing wrong with being headstrong," Claire told him then added, "It's probably your mother's best quality." Claire paused for a second before she got to the crux of her statement. "She told me a few things."

"I can just imagine," he said, bracing himself. "Look, whatever she said, I'm sorry. I didn't put her up to anything. As a matter of fact, I told her not to bother you. But she was never very good at listening to what people were saying. Especially if it wasn't exactly what she wanted to hear."

"Why didn't you tell me that you didn't go on to college because you felt you needed to provide for your mother and your two younger brothers?"

He shrugged, fervently wishing that for once in her life, his mother could have just backed off. He knew that she meant well, but he was already having enough trouble with this estranged situation. He didn't want Claire thinking that he'd deliberately had his mother cite something he had done for his family. He'd done it because he wanted to and felt it was the right thing to do. He hadn't done it to come off as some selfless martyr.

"The subject never came up," he answered vaguely.

For just a moment his answer had rendered Claire speechless. And then she found her tongue.

"The hell it didn't," she retorted. "The subject was there every time I came home from college, every time I'd nag you about going to college yourself."

Levi shrugged, uncomfortable with the very nature of the subject.

"I didn't think you'd be interested in hearing the story," he told her.

The real truth was he was afraid that if Claire knew

the whole story, she might look at him with pity because his father had abandoned him, leaving him to struggle and do the best he could for the ones he cared about.

But in his heart, Levi had felt he owed it to his mother and brothers. That if he could make life a little better for them, then he should. It helped him as much as it did them to make life more tolerable for his family.

The same way he now did for Claire and Bekka.

Right now he just wanted to put this whole subject behind him. "Claire, I know it's late, but I was hoping I could look in on Bekka for a couple of minutes. I promise I won't wake her up."

For a second he thought Claire was going to turn him down. And then she laughed softly.

"You won't have to," Claire told him. "Mother Nature beat you to it. Bekka's been wide-awake for hours now." She looked at Levi for a second. "Maybe she was just killing time while she waited to see her daddy."

He looked at Claire. That certainly didn't sound like the sarcastic, flippant woman he had come to know in the past few weeks. He would have said that he was dreaming—except that he knew he wasn't.

He told himself to stop wasting time before Claire realized that she was being kind and rescinded the implied offer.

"You don't mind if I see her?" he asked uncertainly.

"No, I don't mind," Claire answered in the same quiet voice. She gestured toward the baby lying in the portable playpen. "Go on, it's okay. Since Bekka lights up whenever you walk into a room, maybe it might be a good thing for her if you spent a little time with our little girl."

"Thanks," Levi said to her with feeling. Then he slanted another look toward Claire—a longer one as he tried to puzzle things out—and asked, "How do you feel about my spending time with her mother?"

Claire arched one eyebrow as she regarded him. "I wouldn't push it if I were you, Levi," she warned.

He raised his hands in a sign of complete surrender. "Message received. You don't need to say another word, Claire. My question is officially rescinded," he told her. And then, because he prided himself on always being truthful with Claire, he added, "I'm a patient man. I can wait until you decide to change your mind about that."

Because he had really left her no recourse if she was to save face, Claire told him, "I don't think there's enough patience in the whole world for that."

"We'll see," Levi said softly, more to himself than to her. "We'll see."

Claire gave no indication that she had overheard him. But she had.

And something very deep inside her warmed to his words.

Chapter Nine

"Looks like you're going to be flying solo today, kid," Gene said to his granddaughter when she opened the door to his knock a couple of mornings later.

Gene had become his great-granddaughter's official babysitter while Claire was busy in the kitchen, helping Gina prepare meals for the other residents at the boarding house. Melba told her granddaughter that as far as she was concerned, she was killing two birds with one stone. Bekka was well taken care of while Claire was cooking, and Gene had something meaningful to do that "kept him out from underfoot."

Melba herself saw to it that she was everywhere at once, taking care of the myriad details that went into running the boarding house.

"Ah, there's my little playmate," Gene declared

warmly as he walked into the room and crossed directly to Bekka's portable crib. Half a second later, the baby was in his arms and snug against his chest.

Claire still marveled how her usually crusty grandfather transformed into what amounted to a bowl of mush whenever he was around her daughter. It was as if he became an entirely different person if he got within fifteen feet of the baby.

However, this morning it was what he'd said as part of his greeting that had corralled her attention.

"What do you mean by *solo*, Grandpa? I don't understand." Even so, there was a tight feeling of uneasy anticipation in her stomach.

Patting Bekka's bottom in a soothing motion, Gene obligingly spelled it out for his granddaughter. "Gina called in sick this morning, so you're on your own," he explained. "Who's my best girl?" he asked in the next breath, cooing at the baby in his arms.

Bekka gurgled in response, as if she understood her great-grandfather's question.

"Sick?" Claire repeated. That nauseous feeling was beginning to spread. "What do you mean she called in sick?"

Gently swaying to and fro with the baby, Gene looked at his granddaughter as if he didn't understand exactly what she was questioning.

"Just that. I don't know any other languages to use, Claire-bear. Gina said she was sick and she's not going to be coming in today, so you're in charge of making breakfast, lunch and dinner—since the guests have become accustomed to this. Now do you understand?" he asked.

Her knees suddenly weak, Claire sank down on the edge of her bed just in time. A second later her legs completely turned to liquid.

"Oh, God."

"Hey, it's not so bad," he said, attempting to encourage her. "Your grandmother says you're doing terrific."

Claire raised skeptical eyes to the old man's face. "Grandmother doesn't use the word *terrific* to describe *anything*, much less my halting progress in the world of cooking," she pointed out.

"Okay," Gene conceded reluctantly. "So maybe she didn't use that *exact* word, but she meant that one. You know your grandma. If she's not happy with or about something, we *all* know about it. Fast," he underscored.

Claire still looked stricken about the idea of cooking all those meals by herself. It wasn't that the boarding house was teeming with people, but right now *any* people were just too many for her to deal with.

"I don't even know where to start," she confessed to her grandfather.

"In the kitchen would be a good place," Gene told her with only a hint of a smile on his face. "Come on, princess and I will walk you there, Claire-bear," he offered.

Taking in a shaky breath, Claire let it out slowly. Crossing the threshold, she waited for her grandfather to follow, then locked her door, pocketing the key. "I feel like I'm about to walk my last mile to the execution chamber."

"Have a little faith in yourself, Claire-bear," Gene encouraged.

"I do," Claire countered. "Very little."

As they made their way down the hall to the stairs, Levi opened his door. He was dressed in a light gray suit and blue shirt and was obviously about to leave for work. His attention was instantly captured by the minuscule parade and especially by the distressed look on his wife's face.

Rather than extending a typical greeting to Gene, whom he considered a valuable ally, or pausing to say a few loving words of nonsense to his daughter, his attention was completely focused on Claire.

"Anything wrong, Claire?" Levi asked the inane question, even though he knew there *had* to be something wrong. As a rule, Claire did not sport an expression that looked as if she'd just lost her best friend, but she certainly did now.

Denial immediately rose to her lips, but Claire refrained from saying the words out loud. There'd been a time when she and Levi had been not just husband and wife but best friends, as well, and it was to her former best friend that she now spoke.

"Grandpa just told me that I'm supposed to make breakfast, lunch and dinner for the rest of the boarders today."

Gene had already informed him of Claire's new duties in the kitchen, telling him it was Melba's way of making Claire more domestic. "I thought you were doing that already."

Another shaky breath escaped her lips. "Not by myself, I haven't."

"Gina's sick," Gene volunteered.

"Oh, I see." He searched Claire's face, as if it could answer things for him that she couldn't. "But you've been working with Gina for the last couple of weeks, haven't you?"

There was a world of difference between doing something under watchful, supervising eyes and going it alone as she was now expected to do. "Yes, but—"

Levi didn't let her finish. "Was she satisfied with what you were making?"

Claire raised and lowered her shoulder in a vague response to the question. She felt as if she was on very shaky ground here.

"I guess so…"

He wasn't finished yet. "Did what you made get served?"

She didn't have to think; she remembered each occasion. "Yes."

He smiled, lightly patting her shoulder. "Then you'll be fine."

Claire was far from being sold. "I don't know about that."

It looked as if Claire was going to need more support than just a few encouraging words, Levi thought. He weighed his options, although he already knew what he needed to do. "Tell you what. If you want me to, I'll stick around and help you with breakfast."

"Breakfast is from 7:30 to 9:30," Claire pointed out. That was two hours. More if she factored in the prep time.

"I know," Levi replied.

She expected him to offer a barrage of reasons why he couldn't hold her hand in this, not continue to offer to stay and help. "You'll be late for work." Didn't Levi realize that?

Again he surprised Claire by telling her, "I know that, too."

Was this the same man who was never home? Who seemed to be married to his job and chose it over her time and again? "You're actually willing to do that?" she asked in disbelief. "You're willing to be late for work just to help me out?"

He knew he was risking a lot, but at the same time, if he hadn't proven himself at work yet, then he never would, and there was something really important at stake here. He realized that now.

"You're more important to me than work, Claire." Putting his arm around her shoulders, he said, "Come on, let's go downstairs and get started."

Because he was offering to stay, she didn't feel nearly as threatened by his job as she previously had. Her perspective began shifting.

"No, that's okay," Claire said. "I don't need you to hold my hand. Go to work. You've got a long drive ahead of you."

Reaching the bottom of the stairs, Levi made no move to leave. "You're sure you'll be all right?" he wanted to know.

Claire nodded. There was even a small smile on her lips. "Yes, I'm sure. Besides, I've got a feeling that if I start falling behind, Grandmother will be there to pick up the slack. After all, that was what she used to do and she's too much of a type A personality not to try to take over if she thinks I need help."

"Okay," Levi said, scrutinizing her face closely. "Then I guess maybe I'll see you tonight."

"Maybe," she agreed, echoing what was the key word in his sentence.

He had almost reached the front door when she called after him. "Levi?"

One hand on the doorknob, he turned around to face her. Had she changed her mind about accepting his help after all? "Yes?"

"Thank you."

The smile that bloomed on his lips made his face positively irresistible. It took Claire no effort at all to remember the effect he had had on her when they were first dating. She could remember hardly being able to keep her hands off him—and the feeling had been deliciously mutual.

"Don't mention it," he responded. Nodding at Gene, Levi left the house.

He'd held his peace all during the exchanges between his granddaughter and her husband, but now Gene felt he had to speak his mind. "You ask me, Claire-bear, you married a right nice fella."

She couldn't very well sling mud at her husband right now. "I guess he does have his moments."

Gene chuckled. "That he does, Claire-bear. That he does."

She knew where this was going, and she didn't have time for that discussion. Not the time, nor the heart to try to untangle what had gone wrong with a marriage that looked as if it should have been a triumphant success from day one.

Claire squared her shoulders and turned toward the kitchen in the rear of the first floor. "Yes, Grandpa, but it's the hours I'm thinking about, not the moments. See you after breakfast—I hope."

"Like that boy said—" her grandfather paused to kiss the top of her head "—you'll do just fine. It's breakfast. Nothing special."

"Right," Claire murmured under her breath as she took small, measured steps to the kitchen. "Nothing special."

She had been making breakfast every morning now since her grandmother had put her to work in the kitchen. Melba had taken the mystery out of making French toast, blueberry pancakes and Belgian waffles, as well as showing her a number of different ways to prepare and serve eggs.

That should be more than enough to get her through breakfast.

"I can do this," Claire told herself as she finally walked into the kitchen—a kitchen that for some reason felt a lot bigger this morning than it had on previous mornings. "Get a grip, Claire," she instructed herself sternly under her breath. "You haven't poisoned anyone yet."

She tied her apron on, grabbed her whisk and began cracking eggs.

The second the store was locked up for the evening, Levi all but raced to his car. He was behind the wheel and on the road to Rust Creek Falls less than five minutes after he had double-checked that the security alarms had all been set.

There was a huge bouquet of flowers lying on the passenger seat next to him. In order not to waste any time stopping for them on the way home, he had bought the flowers during part of his lunch break. He'd used the rest of his break to work so that he didn't have to stay after hours, attending to myriad details and making sure that everything was taken care of.

Depending on how the day—meaning her cooking debut—had gone for Claire, the flowers were either to celebrate her success or they were to console her if the meals she made hadn't gone as she'd planned.

Either way, he'd gotten her favorites. Pink and white carnations. A whole avalanche of pink and white carnations. If nothing more, he was hoping to bring a smile to her face—and to help make her see that not only was he on her side, but he was also always thinking of her.

Which he was.

He was also always thinking about their separation. It was going on much too long, and it was beginning to really worry him. Levi was becoming really afraid that if he didn't do something about ending it, it would wind up dragging on much too long and could eventually lead to the one thing he couldn't bear to have happen.

A divorce.

He'd already been painfully rejected once in his life when his father had walked out on his family. While he knew that there had been a number of issues between his parents, issues causing them to argue long and loud, he had taken his father's abandonment of the family personally, feeling that if he had just done something right, said something right, he would have been able to change his father's mind and the man would have remained with them. Would have been the father they all needed.

But he hadn't managed to say something right, *do* something right, and his father had taken off for parts unknown—even to this day. His mother would never say as much, never even so much as *hinted* at this, but he acutely felt that his father's walking out on them had somehow been his fault.

And it all came vividly back to him again when Claire had thrown him out and then, within less than a week, had taken off with the baby to live in another town.

If he hadn't come looking for her, she would have most likely remained where she was and they would now be headed for divorce.

What makes you think you're not still headed there? the devil's advocate in him taunted.

But Levi had to believe otherwise, had to believe that with enough effort on his part, he could turn things around. Could make Claire change her mind about leaving him.

However, even with that effort, even desperately *wanting* to turn things around, for his own sanity he was holding a piece of himself back. It was a gesture of self-preservation. He really couldn't bear to put all of him out there and then, very possibly, get rejected.

If that happened, it would, quite simply, just kill him.

He wasn't brave enough to do that. Not right now. Not yet.

Perhaps not ever.

This way, if she *did* reject him, and he hadn't fully connected with her, then she hadn't rejected all of him because she never *had* all of him.

It was contrived, but it was the only way he had of preserving his peace of mind.

As he drove, Levi kept sipping the triple espresso he had in his cup holder, wanting not just to stay awake but to be wired, as well.

When he reached the boarding house in what amounted to record time for him, Levi felt as if he was ready to go ten rounds with whoever wanted to defend the middleweight boxing championship of the world.

On arrival, he parked at the curb some sixty feet away from the boarding house and all but sprinted to the front door—twice. The first time he was about to enter when he realized that he had left the flowers he had bought for Claire on the seat in his car. He hurried back for the bouquet, then swiftly retraced his steps back to the front door.

Walking in, he was greeted by the lingering, tempting scent of recently fried chicken.

He smiled to himself as he inhaled. It appeared that the flowers he'd brought were going to be of the celebratory nature.

Dinner was over, but he knew for a fact that the refrigerator was not off-limits, at least not for him because he was not only a boarder here at Strickland House, he was also family. Even Melba had grudgingly acknowledged that fact after she'd gotten over old Gene's going behind her back.

Levi peeked into the kitchen, not to see if he could sneak a late meal out of the refrigerator, but to see if Claire was still there.

She wasn't.

That meant, more than likely, that she was upstairs in her room. He'd passed by the common room on his way to the kitchen and hadn't seen her. Process of elimination had put her in her room. Unless she'd gone out for the evening, and he didn't want to entertain that thought unless he really had to.

Levi took the back stairs two at a time, humming and hoping for the best.

Chapter Ten

To Levi's surprise, Claire's grandmother opened the door to Claire's room when he knocked on it.

"Yes?" she asked, her small dark brown eyes taking slow, complete measure of him as she deliberately kept him waiting out in the hall. As far as she was concerned, he had hurt Claire—intentionally or not—and she had yet to forgive him.

She stood blocking access to the room and was also blocking any view into it.

Levi managed to keep down his frustration. "I came to see how Claire's big day went."

Melba's expression was quizzical. "Big day?" she repeated.

"She was doing all the cooking by herself."

"Yes?" she asked expectantly.

"She seemed worried about handling the responsibility, and I just wanted to ask her how it went."

"It went," Melba said with a careless shrug. She was proud of Claire, but too much praise might make the girl relax and stop making the progress she was making lately.

She clearly wanted him to leave, but Levi wasn't ready to do that.

"Well?" he prompted. He tried again to peer into the room, but Melba only moved farther forward, pulling the door behind her.

Cutting off any hope for a view.

"Well, what?" she demanded.

That's not the way he'd meant the word. "Did it go *well* for Claire?"

Melba gave him another nonanswer of sorts. "Her grandfather's taking her out to the movies in Kalispell to celebrate," she said, mentioning the town that was some twenty miles away, "so what do you think?"

"The movies?" Levi echoed in surprise. When they were first dating, he and Claire used to go to the movies regularly. At the time he was thrilled to find out that they actually liked the same kind of films: action movies that still maintained a believable premise. But when the baby had come along, that had all stopped. He began picking up extra hours whenever he could.

He'd done the wrong thing for all the right reasons, he thought now.

"That's what I said."

"Have they left yet?" he asked.

"Yes," Melba told him with finality. "They have."

"No, we haven't," the deep voice behind him told Levi. "Claire was just helping me find my string tie—a man likes to spruce up a bit when he's escorting a pretty lady out in public," Gene explained, and then he chuckled. "But then, I don't have to be telling you that, do I?" he asked Levi.

Standing to one side in order to be able to look at both Levi and his granddaughter who was in the hall behind him, Gene quickly put two and two together and he had a suggestion he felt was in everyone's best interests. Although he had a feeling that Melba wasn't going to be crazy about it. But his wife, in this case, wasn't his first concern.

"Listen, honey," he said to Claire. "As much as I'd love to go to the movies with you tonight, I'm an old man and I'm liable to fall asleep right in the middle of all the excitement. You want to go with someone you can talk with about the movie as you're going home."

"That's okay, Grandpa, we don't have to go," Claire demurred, trying not to look disappointed. It had been a while since she'd had an outing, and the moment her grandfather had suggested it, she'd gotten excited.

"No, I insist you go." He looked at the young man his wife had herded into the hall. "Levi, can I get you to make sure my granddaughter has a good time tonight?"

"Eugene," his wife said sharply, her tone of voice taking him to task and silently threatening him with a whole host of things in that single utterance.

"Yes, sir," Levi replied eagerly.

Gene smiled broadly. "Knew I could count on you, boy. All right, then, it's all settled. And of course the movies are still on me," he added, taking out two bills and pressing them into the palm of Levi's hand. "I insist," he added when Levi opened his mouth to protest. "Now go out and have a good time, you two. Have her tell you all about how good the food turned out today," Gene prompted, all but pushing the two of them together and toward the stairs.

"We need to talk, Gene." Melba all but growled out the words.

"Have an especially good time," Gene instructed his granddaughter and her husband. "Hate to think I did this all for no reason," he added quietly.

"What movie were you going to go see?" he asked Claire as they went down the stairs. In the background, they could hear Melba beginning to berate her husband's "damn fool behavior." Levi cringed inwardly.

"Along Came Jones," Claire answered when they reached the bottom of the stairs. She turned toward him. "Listen, we don't have to do this—"

If their relationship had a chance of healing, Levi knew he was going to have to face things rather than hide his head in the sand, hoping things would work themselves out. It was up to *him* to work them out.

"You don't want to go to the movies with me," he guessed.

"No, that's not it," Claire began.

That was all the lead-in he needed. "Great. Then let's go," Levi told her, brightening.

"You *want* to go?" Claire asked, looking at him uncertainly.

"More than you can possibly ever guess," Levi answered then paused by the front door before opening it. "Why would you ask that?"

She'd had the feeling that things were just disintegrating between them. "Well, Grandpa did seem to twist your arm—"

He stopped her there. "Not that I noticed. We used to do this all the time, remember?" he reminded her, referring to all the movies they had gone to see.

A soft, sentimental smile curved her lips. "I remember," she said almost wistfully. "It seems like a million years ago."

"Not quite that long," Levi replied. And, with any luck, the time line would grow shorter. Taking special care not to ignore her feelings, he told her, "If you don't mind going with me, I'd certainly love to go with you."

Claire recalled his actions just that morning. Levi had been willing to be late for work just to help her out if she asked him to. The offer meant the world to her and had left a very positive impression on her.

She smiled broadly. "Then I guess we're going to the movies."

Levi grinned in response. "I guess so," he agreed. And then he realized that he was still holding the bouquet. "Oh, I almost forgot. These are for you."

She smiled as she looked down into the bouquet. "Carnations. My favorite. I have to put them in water," she told him. "Wait right here," she said. "I'll only be a minute." But before she ran to the kitchen, she paused long enough to brush her lips against his cheek. "Thank you."

And then she hurried off to the kitchen.

She was back in less than five minutes. "All ready," she announced.

"Me, too," he told her.

With his hand at the small of her back, he escorted Claire to his truck. Stopping before the passenger door, he appeared to be a bit self-conscious as he said, "Not exactly a royal coach," even though she had ridden countless times in the truck. He opened the door for her and held it, waiting for her to slide in.

"One person's truck is another person's royal coach," she answered, getting in.

He closed the door then rounded the hood to get in on his side.

Claire waited until he buckled up, then asked him the question that had just occurred to her. "Do you know where the movie's playing?"

"In Kalispell," he replied then assured her, "I'll find it. It hasn't been that long since we've gone to the movies."

"More than a year," she told him, "but I think you'll find it faster if I give you directions."

Levi started up the truck. "Fire away."

As she gave him directions, he smiled to himself. For the duration of this isolated interlude, they were a team again.

There was definitely hope for them, he thought.

* * *

Nearly two and a half hours later, they walked out of the theater, the last of the credits scrolling on the screen as the musical score built up to a final crescendo before the movie screen lightened.

Levi had parked the truck three blocks away out of necessity. All the available parking spaces close to the movie theater had been filled.

As they began to cross the street, Claire stumbled over something. Levi managed to catch her by the hand at the last second, keeping her upright rather than having her unceremoniously sprawl out on the ground.

Caught entirely off balance, Claire sucked air in, her heart temporarily launching into double-time.

His free arm went around her, steadying her further, "You okay?" he asked, his eyes searching her face for signs of acute distress. There weren't any. But there definitely was discomfort.

"I just bruised my pride, nothing else," Claire assured him.

"Maybe you should hold on to me until we get to the truck," Levi suggested. Not waiting for an answer, he tucked her hand through his arm.

She knew he meant well, but this rattled her own self-image. "I'm not an invalid, Levi," she protested.

"Nobody said you were, but there're rocks scattered all around here and it's dark. Do it for my sake," he implored. "If I return you with a turned ankle or worse, more than likely your grandmother's going to skin me— and with great pleasure."

Claire laughed at the exaggeration. "Grandpa wouldn't let her."

He didn't see it that way. "Grandpa, in case you haven't noticed, is afraid of her—just like everyone else is."

"I'm not afraid of my grandmother," Claire informed him. Levi said nothing, but merely continued looking at her. "Very much," Claire finally added.

Levi laughed. "Your grandmother does cast a big shadow for such a little person," he observed.

"She lived in a house with five men. She had to do something to keep from being outnumbered and overwhelmed by them."

"Well, if you ask me, I think she definitely succeeded." Pulling out of the parking spot and then the parking lot, Levi turned the truck toward the Strickland Boarding House. "Almost seemed like old times, didn't it?" he asked Claire. He knew he definitely was having more than just one nostalgic moment.

Claire didn't respond immediately. But when she finally did, she had to grudgingly agree that he had a point. "Almost."

Levi decided to nudge her memory just a tad more. "We used to do this every weekend, remember?"

Claire suppressed a sigh. "I remember. I also remember we used to be younger," she added as if that was reason enough to put the memory away in a deep, dark box.

"Not *that* much younger," Levi insisted.

She begged to differ. But there was another, more important reason why they really couldn't recapture what once was. "And without a daughter to be responsible for."

"That does change things a bit," he had to agree, although if he had a chance to change things, he knew he wouldn't. He dearly loved that little eight-month-old responsibility.

Silence began to take away bits and pieces of the dusky evening. It grew in width and depth until Levi felt he couldn't tolerate it any longer.

"How did it get to be this complicated?" he wanted to know.

She thought that point had already been made. "We had a baby."

"That was supposed to make it better, not complicated," he told her. "There are lots of people with three, four and even five kids."

"Not many," Claire insisted. In this decade, large families were the exception, not the norm.

He disagreed. "Enough."

She closed her eyes, not wanting to get into an argument and spoil what had been, up to this point, a really nice evening. "I don't know how those women do it."

"It's not just the women," he pointed out.

She turned and looked at him. "Ninety-nine percent of the time, yes, it is. The men, if they're in the picture at all, only get to see what life with a kid is like for a limited amount of time. Unless they're stay-at-home dads—something that there's few and far in between— they have no idea what it's like to spend all your time with a crying kid, day in, day out."

She looked at Levi's profile. He was being quiet. Had he even heard what she'd just said? Or was he simply ignoring her?

"Nothing to say?" she asked him.

"I was just thinking," he told her.

She braced herself. "About what?"

He turned to face her. "That maybe we should trade for a day or so."

She didn't understand what he was talking about. "Trade?"

"Yes." The more he thought about it, the more he felt they should give it a shot. "If I gave you a crash course on what I do and my boss okays it, you could come in and do my job, and I'd stay with Bekka and try to do what you do."

She noticed that he hadn't said he could do it, he'd used the word *try*. Did he mean it or was he just attempting to be polite about the situation? And why did he think she needed a crash course in what he did while he could just walk into her life without any effort?

"You sell furniture," she pointed out. "What's so hard about that?"

"I'm the store manager. That entails more than just selling furniture," he told her. He went over only a few of the things he was required to keep tabs on. "That includes payrolls, dealing with customers' complaints and at times their various requirements, as well. It includes making sure that what the customer asks for, he also needs."

He was making it sound complicated. "What does that mean?"

"Well, for instance, I had a couple who wanted to get a five-piece sofa set—wife just fell in love with the model we had on the floor. But their living room was way too small to adequately accommodate it. Which is what I told them after I'd gone to look it over."

She couldn't remember ever getting that kind of service. "You went to their apartment?"

He nodded then explained, "That was all part of the service that helped put my store over the top in sales. I'm not saying that you can't do it, I'm just saying that you can't walk into my job cold. But I could coach you, get you ready—and then if you find that you're into something that you weren't sure how to handle, you could always call me and I'll talk you through it."

That sounded just like him, she thought. But it also didn't sound fair to him. "Isn't that cheating?"

That didn't make any sense to him. "Why would it be cheating? It's only common sense."

He was being so nice, she was starting to feel guilty not only about the way she'd been treating him but even about the way she'd resented him for being able to leave each morning while she felt stuck, tethered to their apartment while dancing attendance to a colicky, teething baby.

She was being quiet again, Levi noted. That wasn't usually a good sign. Luckily, they were home.

He pulled up into an available spot. "We're here," he announced.

Claire blinked. It took a couple of seconds for his words to sink in. When she looked outside the truck, she saw that they had returned to the boarding house without her even realizing it.

It was intensely dark, with only a couple of lights still on within the house. Beyond that, there was no illumination.

They might as well have been the last two people left alive in the world for all the signs of life she saw outside the car window.

Which was possibly why she did what she did next.

Chapter Eleven

Although Levi had parked his truck and turned off the ignition, neither he nor Claire made any attempt to get out of the vehicle.

It was as if they both knew that the second either one of them opened the door on their side and got out, the evening—and the almost magical time that they had just spent with one another, recapturing "old times"—would dissolve into the night.

And when it did, they would once again be that separated couple contemplating the very real possibility of turning their separation into a permanent state by getting a divorce.

Claire didn't want to face any decisions, didn't want to think of what might be ahead or dwell on just what she had already lost and stood to lose if she went forward with her initial threat.

Quite simply, she wanted to preserve this moment in time, wanted nothing more than to have it go on indefinitely.

Wanted, she realized, Levi to want her as much as she found herself wanting him. If possible, she was more attracted to him now, at this moment, than she had been when she'd first met him.

It was with this on her mind that she leaned into Levi. Not by much, but then, considering the limited space around her, it didn't really take all that much. Even a fraction of an inch brought her into his space, brought her closer to his aura.

Taking a steadying breath, she detected just the slightest hint of the soap that Levi favored.

Something clean and woodsy.

His eyes on hers, Levi matched her, small move for small move. Which was how their lips came to occupy almost the exact same space.

They couldn't avoid having them touch.

Ordinarily, given the circumstances, Claire knew she should have pulled her head back, thereby taking her lips out of range and deliberately avoiding his. She would have, with that one simple movement, evacuated the enticing danger zone.

Except that she wanted very much to be in that danger zone. Wanted very much to be kissed by Levi. Wanted, more than anything, to return that kiss a hundredfold.

More.

Her soul had missed him more than any words could begin to describe.

Her heart pounding, she moved *into* the kiss rather than away from it. And, as she moved into it, she kissed her estranged husband with every fiber of her being. Kissed him as if she had never thrown him and her wedding ring out onto the street.

Kissed him as if she still loved him.

Because she did.

Dazed, Levi felt as though he had just been struck by lightning—but he was definitely *not* complaining. If anything, he would have been celebrating and doing handstands—if he wasn't presently and deliciously otherwise occupied.

Very occupied.

Feeling a huge, electrical-like surge throughout his entire body, he leaned in over the truck's gearshift, taking no note of it as he took Claire into his arms.

Holding on to her because letting her go meant losing his soul.

Levi could feel his body heating up, could feel himself yearning for Claire the way he hadn't thought was humanly possible. A very large part of him felt that he wouldn't be able to breathe if he couldn't have her.

Get a grip, Levi, he sternly upbraided himself.

He didn't want to be guilty of overpowering her. Of making her succumb to the moment if she was only going to regret it later. There was more than just sex involved here, and he didn't want her thinking that *that* was what was foremost in his mind.

As much as his body felt incomplete without being sealed to hers, he didn't want to risk losing her permanently if he let her believe that all he wanted was to make love with her and that he would do anything that was necessary, would move any obstacle that might be in his way, to *get* his way with her.

He loved her too much for that.

And it was that very love that made him vulnerable to her.

Claire felt herself weakening more and more by the second. Within a couple more seconds, she knew she'd be all ready and primed to be taken by him right here, never mind that they were parked in front of her grandparents' boarding house.

There was too much riding on this for her to completely give in to the demands she felt inside. Doing so would only cloud the issue—attaining a better relationship in which they could communicate well enough to be able not to have things blow up between them the way they had since the July Fourth wedding. So she kissed the only man she had ever truly loved once more for the road—a very steamy, rocky road—and then she pulled back, albeit very reluctantly.

Clearing her throat so that she could sound like a human being when she spoke, rather than squeaking, Claire whispered, "I think we'd better be going in."

She was right.

He knew she was right, even as every muscle in his

body loathed to back away. But there was no way, no matter how he felt, that he was about to force himself on her. It didn't matter that she was his wife, that in their brief time together they had made love countless times and with utter, complete abandon.

That was then, this was now.

This time around, she had backed away, indicating, by example, that he had to do the same. He wasn't about to cast a shadow on what they'd had—what he hoped they *would* have again—by pretending not to hear her or just getting it into his head to override her and simply take what was his.

Because that would destroy what they'd had and what he wanted them to have again.

Much as it pained him down to the very bottom of his soul, there were new rules to follow—and Levi was determined that he was going to follow them. This while fervently praying that she would come back to him soon because holding out this way for long was bordering on sainthood.

"Whatever you want, Claire," he replied solemnly.

Whatever I want, Claire thought, repeating his words in her head.

What I want is to rip your clothes off with my teeth and have you do the same to mine.

What I want is to make wild, passionate love with you until neither one of us can breathe.

What I want is for none of this to have ever happened so that we could just go on the way we had once been.

But that wasn't the reality they were faced with,

Claire was forced to admit. She *had* thrown him out, and she *had* pulled up stakes and moved away with Bekka. She couldn't just undo that in the blink of an eye without looking like some kind of a flighty, bird-brained idiot. Why would he want to stay with a flighty, quick-tempered woman, even if her makeup was always perfectly applied and she never had a hair out of place?

The simple answer was that he wouldn't.

Pulling herself together, burying her desire until such time as she could effectively handle it and perhaps even give it a voice in her life, Claire nodded in response and opened the door on her side.

It would have been helpful if a blast of cold air had hit her, making her shiver and focus on trying to keep warm. But this was August, so the only air she detected was on the hot side, and it was more of a waft than a blast.

That was all she needed. The sensation of heat traveling up and down her body— reminding her how she had felt whenever Levi touched her and made her his.

Closing the passenger door behind her, Claire let out a long, shaky breath. And then she squared her shoulders and headed for the boarding house front door. She heard Levi getting out behind her on the driver's side.

"You don't have to walk me to my door," she told him without turning around.

Her very real fear was that if he came in with her, somehow or other, she would wind up pulling him into her room, ruining all her good intentions.

"I'm not," Levi answered. When she turned to look

at him quizzically, as if she had just caught him in a lie, he pointed out, "I live here, too, remember?"

She'd actually forgotten for a second. What was the matter with her? She was too young to be courting senility.

Apparently, Claire decided, her rampant desires were wiping out everything else, including what there was of her thought process.

"Yes," she replied quietly. "I remember."

The hall light was the only lamp lit on the first floor, a clear indication that everyone had either gone to bed— or was making an evening of it somewhere else.

Claire went up the stairs to her room.

She was aware of Levi following her up the stairs. She knew he was just going to his room, which was down the hall from hers, but even so, she was waging a battle within herself, wrestling with the pros and cons of inviting Levi into her room for just a few minutes to see the baby. After all, it was his right.

Claire knew that he and Bekka would both enjoy the interaction. No matter what went down between her and Levi, good and bad, she couldn't deny that he was a fantastic father and that Bekka still lit up like a lighthouse beacon whenever he walked into their daughter's room.

But in her own present state, Claire thought, she lit up, as well.

Maybe even more so, Claire thought in semidespair.

Turning at the top of the stairs, in this position she was eye to eye with Levi. "If Bekka's awake, do you want to stop in for a minute and see her before you go to bed?"

It was *his* turn to light up like that lighthouse beacon.

"If you don't mind," he prefaced. "Sure."

He had to admit, ever since she had thrown him out, he was carrying around a very real fear that even if they got back together, she could easily reject him again. He had to safeguard himself from that.

Because emotionally he just couldn't bear another rejection.

Claire looked at him, puzzled. "Why should I mind? I just asked if you wanted to. If I *minded*, I wouldn't have made the offer."

"No," he agreed, thinking it over. She wouldn't play games where Bekka was concerned. "I guess you wouldn't have. Thanks," he told her with a wide smile.

Levi could always undo her with his smile. "Don't mention it," she murmured, feeling her heart beating in triple time.

The first thing she saw the second she unlocked her door was her grandfather. Gene quickly crossed over and told her in a whisper, "She just dropped off to sleep about ten minutes ago. That means you can get in about two hours of uninterrupted sleep before she's ready to roll again." Her grandfather looked from his granddaughter to the young man who had brought her back. "I suggest you make the most of it," he said just before he slipped out of the room.

It wasn't clear just who Gene was giving that advice to.

Levi took her grandfather's exit to mean that he should be leaving, as well.

"Well, I guess then I'd better—" Levi began, about to back out of Claire's room.

"You can still look at her if you'd like to," Claire told him. "It might even be a little easier to look at her with her asleep. This way she's not bouncing all over the place."

"You might have a point there," Levi said just before he tiptoed over to his daughter's crib. Leaning his arms on the railing, he looked down at the little girl's face. "She looks just like an angel, doesn't she?" he whispered to Claire as he continued gazing at the sleeping, cherubic face.

"God's clever use of deceptive packaging," Claire replied, amusement curving the corners of her generous mouth.

"Bekka will grow out of it and calm down," Levi predicted. "In about five years or so—give or take," he added with a fond laugh. It was obvious that no matter what she did and how old she got, she would always be his little girl, and he'd love her unconditionally.

Which made Bekka, Claire thought, one lucky little girl. And by association, that made her lucky, as well, to have that kind of a loving father for her child.

"Hope you're right," Claire told him. They both stood there, looking down on what amounted to their most precious handiwork, for several moments.

When Levi took her hand in his, her breath caught in her throat. For a second she was afraid to move, afraid of encouraging him—more afraid of doing something to discourage him and chase Levi away.

"Gene said something about her staying asleep for a couple of hours. Does she?" Levi questioned.

Claire nodded. "Bekka's taken to sleeping for two hours at a time. She just started doing that the last couple of weeks. I was stunned," she admitted. "But thrilled at the same time."

"Then I guess you'd better listen to Gene and make the most of it. I should let you get your rest," Levi told her. "I'll see you in the morning," he added, forcing himself to cross to the door.

A sense of urgency washed over her. "Levi—"

When he turned around to look at her and hear whatever last minute words she wanted to send him off with, he found that he didn't have very far to look. Claire was right there, standing right inside his shadow.

"Claire?"

Even the way he said her name excited her.

In the very next heartbeat, she wrapped her arms around his neck, pushed herself up on her toes and then sealed her mouth to his.

Levi resisted.

Or at least he thought he did. That part transpired in far less than a heartbeat, after which time every noble intention he'd gathered together to help him stay strong and rise above his desires was utterly and effectively stripped away from him.

Before he knew what he was doing, Levi kissed her

back. Part of him, a very small part, still struggled to do the right thing and pull back.

When he finally succeeded in creating a small space between them, he'd only been able to draw his head back a couple of inches from hers.

"Claire, are you sure—?"

"Stop talking," she instructed breathlessly.

Claire had no idea if she was strong enough to override the kind of logic he might throw at her. All she knew was that her whole body was burning for him. It felt as if it was vibrating like a freshly struck tuning fork, all because of the very delicious feel of his body pressed against hers.

She had no doubt that come morning, she was going to regret this.

Perhaps a little.

Most likely a lot.

But right now what she would definitely regret was letting him return to his room, leaving her to crawl into her own bed.

Alone.

Heaven help her, she *needed* him.

Chapter Twelve

The ache that came over Levi, instant and acute, reminded him of every single second that he had gone without making love with Claire. But despite the keenly felt desire, a shaky but irrefutable logic still managed to prevail.

For the second time in as many minutes, he drew his lips away from Claire's, leaving her confused and bereft, if the expression on her face was any indication of what she was experiencing.

"The baby," he murmured thickly.

Claire instantly understood what he was referring to, understood the conscientious objection that he was raising.

Moving over to the crib, which was no longer located right next to her bed as it had been when she'd left for the movies—her guess was that her grandfather had had a premonition about the way the evening might wind up going and with that in mind had moved the crib as far away from her bed as possible—she picked up the baby blanket and spread it out so that it covered the entire length of the guard rail.

Spread out this way, the pink blanket would provide the only viewing surface Bekka would be able to look at if the baby should open her eyes while she and Levi were otherwise occupied.

Turning from the now-isolated crib, Claire smiled at the man who had won her heart just a few years ago, her smile clearly indicating that the mission was accomplished.

His concerns about Bekka laid to rest, Levi wasted no time pulling his wife back into his arms. Capturing her lips again, his hands eagerly roamed over all the stirring curves of her body.

Levi worshipped every inch of her and happily celebrated the very thought of their physical reunion to come.

"I've missed this," he breathed against the side of her throat, his breath quickly stirring her to an unimaginable fever pitch. "I've missed *you*, Claire."

Eager for that special form of frenzy that only he could create within her, Claire pushed Levi back against her bed, and quickly began tearing at his shirt, working his belt loose and then urgently tugging at his slacks, drawing them down off his taut hips and hard, muscular thighs.

She had him half-undressed before he had pulled down her tank top and the strapless bra that she wore beneath it.

Her shorts came next, leaving her in what could be rated as the skimpiest of all-but-transparent hot-pink thong panties.

The thong's life expectancy swiftly plummeted down to zero in less than thirty seconds as he slid his fingertips beneath the thin elastic on either side of her hips. And then, in the blink of an eye, the thong and her hips parted company, and she was lying on top of him, completely nude.

Wrapping his arms around her and covering her mouth with his own, Levi reversed their positions and she was suddenly beneath him.

He took great care to balance his weight on the length of his arms and his elbows even as his lips reacquainted themselves with the length and breadth of her skin.

Levi kissed her everywhere, making her head spin, her heart race and her body prime itself for him. The yearning she experienced was almost unbelievably urgent and ever so overwhelming.

She wasn't sure just how she managed to get the remainder of his clothes away from his body, but she finally accomplished that, eager to give as good as she got.

But Levi had always been the master at this game. She had come to him with limited experience, and he had uncovered such mind-blowing pleasures for her that she knew without being told that what she had with Levi was something indescribably precious and wonderful.

Levi kept on kissing her until he had reduced her to a pulsating mass of desire. And then she felt his lips withdrawing from hers only to leave their imprint on her neck, her shoulders, the swell of her breasts and then her newly taut belly.

The muscles quivered beneath his lips and hot, stirring breath. Claire arched into his lips, eager to absorb every nuance, every pass that he made.

Levi went farther down.

Deeper.

Priming her soft, inner core, his tongue wove magic, creating havoc even as it coaxed one climax after another from her.

It was all sweet agony.

Claire chewed on her lip. It was all she could do not to cry out. Only the fact that her cries would wake up the baby held her in check.

Grabbing fistfuls of bedding in her hands as she tried to anchor part of herself to reality, Claire arched higher and higher, eager to experience the full impact of the sensations that Levi was so expertly creating within her.

She fell back, exhausted, only to feel his lips forging a path back up to hers. Claire was sure that there was nothing left within her, nothing to give, nothing to absorb.

She was miles beyond tired.

And then he moved her legs apart with his knee and entered her.

Levi did it slowly, gently, as if he didn't want to take a chance on hurting her even though they had made love this way countless times before, often several times in the space of a few hours.

And yet, she realized, Levi treated her like a virgin bride.

And in so doing, he'd caused her to fall in love with him all over again.

Almost in slow motion, Levi managed to create paradise for her, bringing her closer and closer to the ultimate climax, the ultimate moment that they could both share.

She didn't want slowly.

Claire raced to that wondrous sensation eagerly, knowing that Levi was there to share it with her, to feel everything she was feeling.

That made it twice as special as it had been before.

Clinging to him, Claire climbed up to the very pinnacle of the mountain they were trying to scale.

And then, just like that, they skydived down back to the ground together.

Claire clung to him on the way down, as well, unwilling to give up even a second of the experience or draw into herself before it was time.

She truly wanted to have him there, beside her, guiding her and protecting her. Doing all the things that had made her fall in love with him in the first place.

When the euphoria finally abated, moving back into the shadows, Claire was more than a little reluctant to release her hold on it.

But whether or not she did it, the sensation still receded, vanishing into the ether until there wasn't even a trace of it left.

Claire sighed, burying her face in Levi's shoulder, not wanting to engage with the world just yet.

Levi could feel her turning into him, could feel him wanting her in response. He felt every breath she took and released.

Damn, but she was stirring up things again, making him want her again.

Making him ready to stay the night and pick up all the threads of his life and arrange them the way they had once been.

Closing one arm around his wife to keep her against him, Levi kissed the top of her head. "I have *missed* that," he murmured with great feeling into her hair.

Raising her head ever so slightly so that she could look up at him, Claire said in a hushed whisper, "Me, too."

He wanted to keep on talking, to somehow get her to tell him—no, to promise him—that his period of exile from her life was over. That she was willing to pick up and resume their lives just where they had left them.

To hear that would have meant the world to him, perhaps even put his uneasiness to rest, at least for a while. But he knew that if he said any of this to her, it left him open to the possibility that she could say no, then continue to say that nothing had really changed between them despite this quick visit to happier days.

Because if she said that, it would most likely crush

him, and right now he was far too vulnerable to risk that. He hadn't managed to properly build up his walls, his defenses against the possibility of hearing things that would leave devastating holes in his soul.

So he said nothing and just held her in his arms for as long as he could.

The silence enveloped her.

At first she thought nothing of it. But ever so slowly, it began to make her feel uncomfortable.

Awkward.

Made her feel as if, now that the sexual tension had been addressed and depleted for the time being, they were suddenly being thrown back to the lives they'd been living a few short hours ago.

"Is something wrong?" she heard herself finally asking him.

"No," Levi denied a bit too quickly, belying his thought process. "Why? Do you feel something's wrong?" he asked, throwing the ball back into her court.

"You're not talking."

"Funny, I thought I heard myself talking. I could have sworn that was the sound of my voice just now. Oh, wait, there it goes again," he said, hoping to get his point across to Claire. To make her laugh.

Instead of amused, Claire looked a little frustrated. "You know what I mean."

"No," Levi was forced to admit since he didn't believe in lying. "Not usually."

She propped herself up on her elbow to look at him from a better angle. "We just made love."

"I know," he replied with a solemn expression. "I was there."

"And now you're pulling back," she pointed out.

He balked at the criticism, even though he knew, in his heart, that she was right. "I'm right here," he contradicted.

"Physically," Claire emphasized. Didn't he see the difference? "I'm talking about what you have inside." She jabbed an index finger into his chest.

Levi fell back on logic, the way he always did. "What I have inside is a whole bunch of organs, which still seem to be working at maximum capacity."

She closed her eyes and sighed. Opening them again, she said, "I'm talking about your spirit."

"Spirit," he repeated. "As in ghosts?"

Levi was deliberately baiting her, wanting to see where this was going and just what she truly felt about what had happened. Because he would have liked nothing more than to hear that this meant they were going to get back together. That she missed them being a couple as much as he did.

He was well aware that in each relationship, one person always loved more than the other. It was a given as far as he was concerned. But what he couldn't bear was if it turned out that he was the only one in this relationship. He wouldn't be able to stand it if she was going to turn her back on him and willfully abandon him the way his father had.

He knew he wouldn't be able to live with that or bear up to that.

"No, not as in ghosts," she said, a slight glimmer of anger creasing her brow, tainting her reaction to him and to what had just happened here between them. "As if what we're both carrying within us—what makes us fall in love," she added before he could jump back on that ridiculous analogy about inner organs and whatnot, "doesn't really exist." She drew herself up, holding the sheet against her breasts. "Didn't you *ever* love me?" she wanted to know.

"Of course I did—I do," he amended when he realized that he'd framed his answer using the past tense. All he was doing was following her lead, but he knew if he pointed that out, she'd lash out at him, claiming that he was just being argumentative.

Claire looked unconvinced—but she also looked as if she *wanted* to be convinced.

"If you love me, why did you go off that night to play poker with the guys instead of coming home with me to *play* something else?"

At this point he honestly didn't know, but saying that sounded like a cop-out, so he tried to come up with something that sounded plausible.

"You were busy," he began, thinking of the woman at the wedding that Claire had been talking to.

"I have never been too busy for you—unlike you for me," she said with renewed feeling.

"*When* was I ever too busy for you?" he wanted to know.

Was he kidding? "Almost every day—when you

don't come home from work," she added, in case he was too obtuse to understand her meaning.

"That's just it. Work. It's *work*, it's not personal—"

She sniffed, showing contempt for his answer, clearly unconvinced. "It certainly felt personal to me. And it would to you, too, if *you* were on the receiving end of what I've had to put up with," she informed him.

It was happening, Levi thought.

He could feel it.

They were slipping back into the quagmire comprised of her grievances about his behavior. If he didn't get up and leave now, she was just going to start going over the entire litany of his faults and shortcomings.

The second she started, any headway that he'd felt being made while they were making love would swiftly become null and void—as if it had never happened, he thought. He would rather leave now and retain a shred of what he felt had transpired between them than to stick around and watch it all come crashing down and burn.

Again.

Sitting up, he swung his legs down on the opposite side of the bed, rose and began picking up his clothing. He began to pull on his slacks and shirt.

Levi was dressed within a couple of minutes.

Claire remained sitting up in bed, watching him. Stunned and speechless. When she finally found her tongue, she demanded, "What do you think you're doing?"

He spared her a fleeting glance. "Putting my clothes on."

She could see that. What she wanted from him was to know *why* he was putting his clothes on.

"Just like that?" she demanded.

"Only way I know how to get dressed," he said, his voice devoid of feeling.

Her eyes narrowed. "That's not what I meant."

He shrugged. "Guess you're just going to have to work on being able to communicate your thoughts better."

He was criticizing her. They'd just made love and she'd thought—she'd thought—

Angry tears filled her eyes,

Damn, nothing had been resolved, she told herself. She was a fool to think that a few loving moments made everything all right.

"Get out," she ordered, pointing at the door. To underscore her command, she threw a pillow at him.

He ducked out of the door and closed it before the pillow could come in contact with him.

Chapter Thirteen

Claire had thrown him out.

Again.

Levi knew in his gut that it was just a matter of time before she would issue a full-scale rejection, banishing him from her life just as she had after that blasted wedding they'd attended.

Except that this time it could very possibly be permanent.

And if that happened, she would be, in essence, abandoning him.

Abandoning him just the way that his father had abandoned him.

Because he wasn't worth loving.

Wasn't worth sticking around for and trying to iron

out the snags that had occurred in the fabric of their relationship.

And he obviously wasn't worth the effort to even *attempt* to set things right.

It was the story of his life, Levi thought glumly as he sat in the dark in his room. He might as well bail rather than stick around and have the point driven home that much more sharply.

Even so, it still hurt, he thought. It hurt like hell.

It was his fault, Levi realized, staring into the darkness. His fault for thinking that he could actually have a woman like Claire in his life. His fault for thinking that a woman like Claire could love him—and that he had an actual shot at building a solid life with her and their daughter.

On some level, he'd known all along that this was liable to happen.

That was why he'd done what he could to consciously hold a piece of himself back when they made love. Because if he held back, then maybe he wouldn't be completely destroyed if she turned her back on him and left him again.

All in all, it was a decent protective, working theory. But in reality, his defense mechanisms weren't nearly as effective as he needed them to be.

He still felt vulnerable and completely stripped down to his skin.

He was just going to have to harden himself, because as long as he remained in the Strickland Boarding House, there was a good chance that he and Claire would run into each other, that their paths would cross no matter how careful he was to keep away from her.

His path, Levi thought, was clear. He was going to have to pack up and leave as soon as he got back from work tomorrow.

But the following evening, when he arrived back at the boarding house, Levi felt far too exhausted to face the prospect of packing, so he put off leaving the boarding house—and Claire—until the following day.

But the evening that followed that one brought with it the same set of circumstances, the same reluctance on his part and consequently, the same results.

So did the day after that.

And the day after that.

Levi made peace with the idea that he wasn't going anywhere for a while, telling himself that it was easier to do nothing and remain in limbo, than to take an inevitable step that would, he felt, irrevocably close a chapter of his life. A chapter, he was sure, he would never be able to open again.

Claire slipped back into her room. Breakfast was finally over. She'd been working on automatic pilot for days now, and she was drained.

Her room was empty and so quiet, the silence all but vibrated around her as well as within her. Her grandfather, bless him, had happily taken over the care and feeding of Bekka, as he did every day while she went off to the kitchen to help feed the masses.

She was very grateful for his help, but as her grandmother had pointed out, he enjoyed caring for Bekka and playing with her, so it wasn't exactly a hardship for him to watch the baby. Besides, it made him feel useful, as well as happy.

Claire had to admit that she envied her grandfather his happiness.

Happiness.

It was something she felt that she would never experience again. Finding out that she'd been right all along in her dealings with Levi didn't make her feel the slightest bit better or vindicated.

This was one time she would have given *anything* to have been wrong. But Levi had proven that she'd been right by his glaring absence from her life.

Ever since she was in her teens, she'd been insecure when it came to her looks. Marriage didn't change anything. It certainly didn't change her thinking. All along she had felt that she wasn't pretty enough to hold on to a man like Levi.

Levi was sharp, clever and so handsome that it almost hurt. What would he want with someone like her? Why would he tie himself down with her? Especially long-term? In a desperate effort to ensure that he would remain in her life, she had gone out of her way to be certain that Levi would never see her without her makeup on, or with her hair uncombed—not even once.

A case in point was the day she had gone into labor. She hadn't called him to take her to the hospital before she had checked her hair and her makeup in the mirror—and touched up her lipstick as well as spraying a fine mist of cologne into her hair. She wanted to look picture-perfect each and every time he looked at her.

So that he wouldn't be tempted to leave her.

Granted, that did make her life that much harder, but she'd wanted to be sure that if he left—as he now indeed had—it wouldn't be because he wanted to find someone more attractive than she was.

But it seemed now that he had grown tired of her anyway.

Even when they had made love that last time, here at the boarding house, she had felt that Levi was definitely holding back, holding a part of himself in check, just out of her reach.

She had wanted to give Levi her all, but after sensing that, she had suddenly shut down and backed away herself.

Two could play the "stranger" game, she thought. If Levi wanted to treat her like someone he barely knew, well, she could do the same with him.

But behaving this way was taking a terrible toll on her, making her usually sunny disposition all but vanish entirely. She managed to sound upbeat when dealing with some of the other residents in the boarding house. And she was fairly certain that she had fooled her grandfather and even her more suspicious grandmother, but it was far from easy.

Which was why she was here in her room, seeking out a little space and trying very hard to rally her spirits which had, over the past few days, plummeted down to a subbasement level.

Thinking of what she'd had and now apparently had lost, Claire couldn't keep the tears from surfacing. However, since she was alone, she let them come, hoping to get all the sadness out of her.

Claire threw herself facedown on her bed, gathered her pillow to her and just cried. She stifled her sobs by burying her head in her pillow.

She wasn't sure just how long she remained like that, crying her heart out. She knew that she'd cried so hard and so long, she was virtually exhausted.

That was when she heard the knock on her door.

Caught off guard, she remained silent, hoping that whoever was on the other side of the door would think she wasn't in and would just go away.

But they didn't go away.

The second round of knocking had her pulling into herself even more, determined to wait it out. The last thing she felt like doing was talking.

To anyone.

Shutting her eyes, she braced herself to wait the person out.

She wasn't prepared for the door to suddenly be opened.

The second it began to move, Claire popped up into a sitting position. She rubbed the heels of her hands against her eyes, trying to clear away as much as she could of the telltale trail of tears.

She was just lucky she wasn't one of those women

who spent a great deal of time on her eye makeup. If she had, she was certain she would have looked like a raccoon right now. Instead, at most, she would be showing some puffiness beneath her eyes, which could mean any one of a number of things, not necessarily a sign of the heartbreak she was experiencing.

The next second, her grandmother walked in, pocketing her pass key.

"Why aren't you answering your door?" Melba Strickland wanted to know.

Scowling, with one hand on her ample hip, the woman looked very formidable despite her short stature.

Claire looked down at the rumpled bedspread on the bed. "Sorry," she mumbled. "I guess I must have fallen asleep and didn't hear you."

The scowl on Melba's face deepened more than just a fraction.

"Okay, then." Melba sniffed, closing the door behind her. Coming into the room, she took her granddaughter's chin in her hand and carefully scrutinized both sides of her face. "And just when, exactly, did you take up lying to your grandmother?" she wanted to know.

Nerves caused adrenaline to go surging through her system. She wasn't any good at this, but since she'd laid the groundwork, she felt she needed to see it through. "I'm not lying. I'm…"

"Experiencing a lapse in good judgment?" Melba supplied.

Feeling very vulnerable in her present position—she

was looking up at her grandmother as if she were down on her knees—Claire got off her bed.

"Is there something I can do for you, Grandmother?" she asked, doing her best to sound calm.

"Yes," the woman answered in a no-nonsense tone of voice. "You can stop feeling sorry for yourself."

Claire's defenses went into high gear. "I'm not feeling sorry for—" Claire stopped. Oh, what was the point of trying to deny it? Her grandmother had this eerie ability to see right through her. "How can you tell?"

Melba snorted. "I'm old and I've seen it all, Claire-bear." Narrowing her eyes, the older woman stared at her granddaughter's face again. "This have anything to do with that exiled husband of yours?" she asked.

Claire waited a couple of beats before asking, "If I said no, would you believe me?"

Melba's eyes held hers. Her face was devoid of any telltale expression. "What do you think?"

She knew her grandmother well enough to give up any attempt at denial. "Then I won't say no."

Melba nodded her head. "Good thinking. And speaking of thinking—or not thinking—just what is going on with you two?" Melba asked. Her tone indicated that she wouldn't put up with any attempts to weasel out of answering her. "A week ago, it looked as if things were getting back on track between you and Levi. Now you're involved in some kind of elaborate game of hide-and-seek—except that neither one of you is seeking." When Claire didn't say anything, Melba ordered, "Out with it."

It was useless to beat around the bush. So she didn't. "He doesn't want me anymore."

"Honey, if that were the case, that man would have been long gone. Nobody's holding a gun to his head, making him stay here—and he *is* still here," her grandmother pointed out.

Sitting down on Claire's bed, the woman looked expectantly at her until Claire followed suit and sat back down on the bed beside her.

"Let me make myself clear," her grandmother began. "Levi Wyatt wouldn't have been my first choice for you—or my second, for that matter. But he does seem to be crazy about Bekka, and any fool can see that man loves you. Ever since you've crawled into that shell of yours, your furniture cowboy seems to have gotten downright mopey. Now, just what makes you think that he doesn't love you anymore?"

Claire took a breath as she looked away. "I'm just not pretty enough," she muttered.

"What?" Melba said sharply.

As if this was easy for her to admit, Claire thought. But she knew that her grandmother would just chip away at her until she had the whole story. Telling her the story right off the bat was just saving her a lot of grief.

"I tried very hard to look perfect for him—I've never let him see me without my makeup. Not even once," Claire said with just a touch of pride. "But that doesn't seem to be enough. I'm just not pretty enough or interesting enough to hold on to him."

Melba stared at her for a moment that grew so long, it became almost intolerable.

And then she spoke. "So what you're telling me is that you married a shallow jerk."

"No!" Claire cried, horrified at the label her grandmother had just slapped on Bekka's father. "He's not a shallow jerk!"

Melba looked far from convinced. "Well, only a shallow jerk is going to stop loving someone because they decided that the woman they married wasn't as *pretty* as they thought she was. Is Levi *that* shallow?" her grandmother wanted to know, her sharp brown eyes pinning Claire down, daring her to defend the indefensible.

"No, he's not," Claire declared loyally. "But I'm still not pretty enough to hang on to him."

Melba sighed, shaking her head. Her granddaughter had *so* much to learn. "Honey, there are a lot of things that go into making and maintaining a good marriage— being pretty doesn't even make the top twenty. Surface beauty doesn't last, and unless it goes beyond being skin-deep, being pretty is not good for anything except maybe making makeup commercials.

"Now, that young man you married is not a rocket scientist, but he's pretty sharp, which means he's got a good head on his shoulders and some decent set of values to guide him." Her grandmother's eyes held hers. "The man doesn't want a picture-perfect wife. He wants a loving wife. One he can talk to and reason with.

"There's no such thing as perfect anyway. Best you can hope for is someone who tries their best to be a good husband—or a good wife," Melba said pointedly, looking at her granddaughter. "Now, let me let you in on a little secret. Marriages aren't made in heaven. They're made right here on earth and played out here, as well.

"Nothing good is ever gotten easily. You have to work at it, fight for it, sacrifice for it. That's when you really get to appreciate what you have. Someone hands you something on a silver platter, you might like it and enjoy it for a little while, but that doesn't come close to the way you feel after you've fought the good fight and won something. It also becomes a lot more precious to you. Now, stop hiding in your room and see if you can make that young man want to go on putting up with you."

Claire wished she could, but the sinking feeling in her stomach told her there was no point in even trying. "It's too late."

Melba rose to her feet. Holding her granddaughter's hand, she brought Claire up with her. "It's only too late if one of you is dead, and unless he's expired on his way to work, your man is alive and well and coming back here tonight. The only way that man is going to leave you is if you chase him away. So *stop chasing him away.*"

Claire shook her head. "You're wrong. I can feel him holding back—"

"Well, yeah," Melba agreed. "Of course he's holding back. If you thought someone was going to use your heart for flamenco practice, you'd hold back, too.

"Look, you've already declared your marriage

dead—you've got nothing to lose by approaching Levi, and everything to gain." When her granddaughter made no move to leave the room, Melba delivered her ultimate threat. "Just remember, you're not too big for me to take over my knee."

Claire laughed shortly, thinking her grandmother was kidding. "I'm not a kid anymore, Grandmother," she pointed out. "I'm an adult."

"You're an adult," the older woman echoed. Melba's eyes narrowed again as she focused in on her granddaughter. "Fine. Then prove it."

Chapter Fourteen

Claire looked at her grandmother, confused. "I don't understand. What do you mean, *prove it*? What are you telling me to do?"

Melba huffed, exasperated. Shutting the door again, she proceeded to answer her granddaughter's question. "I'm telling you to *act* like an adult. When Levi comes home tonight, go up to him and apologize for your part in this fiasco that's gotten so completely out of hand. Own up to your mistakes—it takes two to have an argument, not just one person."

Frowning, her eyes swept over Claire. "And for heaven's sake, let him see you the way you really are, not like this." She waved her hand to indicate Claire in her entirety. "Not like some girl who's ready to be on the cover of some fashion magazine. If he loves you, then he loves *you*, not your shade of lipstick, or the eye shadow you have on." Melba's gaze was highly disapproving. "Or that powder you use to hide any so-called flaws you think you have.

"The man married *you*, not a makeup case. Give him a little credit," Melba insisted, surprising Claire. She'd been under the impression that her grandmother did *not* approve of Levi. This sounded as if she was in his corner. "Besides," Melba continued, "there's nothing wrong with the way you look. What *is* wrong is your insecurity."

Melba abruptly stopped herself from going on. "Now, despite what you're probably thinking, I'm not here to lecture you. I just want to wake you up to what you stand to lose if you don't get a grip on your behavior." Blowing out a breath, Melba glanced at her wristwatch. "Time for you to stop feeling sorry for yourself and get back to the kitchen, Cinderella. Until she's feeling better, Gina's going to need your help."

Melba opened the door and stepped out into the hallway. Claire was quick to pull herself together and follow her out of the room. "And while you're working," Melba added as a parting shot. "*Think* about what I just said. Think very, very hard."

"Yes, ma'am," Claire murmured.

Heading in a different direction than her granddaughter, Melba spared her one last look and just shook her head without saying another word.

Claire had no idea how to read her grandmother's parting expression, but the woman had certainly given her a great deal to think about. She supposed that her grandmother did have a point. She had married a man, a *real* man, not some prince charming who only existed in fairy tales.

Since he was real, she owed it to Levi to let him see her the way she really looked. He'd earned the right. Levi had followed her here even after she'd thrown him out. That *had* to count for something, she reasoned. Maybe he did really love her and not just the image she had been projecting every day and night since that first day that they met.

It wasn't Levi who had set her on this path of always projecting a picture-perfect image. She had been like this ever since she could remember. She had never allowed herself to appear dirty or messy in public, never left the house unless she passed her own inspection, critically looking herself over in a full-length mirror.

What that amounted to was always being neat, always making sure that her clothes, her makeup and her hair were all impeccable. The idea of looking anything less than exceedingly attractive was just unthinkable to her. She didn't even own a pair of sweatpants or a pair of sneakers.

Her grandmother was right, Claire thought grudgingly. It was time to let her hair down.

In more ways than one.

Claire began to watch the clock, counting the hours and the minutes until Levi came back to the boarding house from the furniture store. Although it had taken a lot of courage, she had made up her mind. She was going to unveil herself, to show Levi the *real* Claire, flaws and all.

And then she was going to pray that he didn't find the real her a turnoff.

Levi stared straight ahead at the dark road in front of him. With little or no traffic before him, the road was numbingly hypnotic. The second he had hit the road tonight, he'd made up his mind.

This was going to be the last time he'd make this run.

It was time to face the facts, pick up his marbles and, in effect, "go home." There was no point in continuing to beat his head against the wall. It wasn't going to change anything, wasn't going to give him the outcome he'd been hoping for.

He and Claire weren't going to get back together again.

For him to pretend otherwise was just another way of prolonging his pain. He'd been stalling these past few days, stubbornly and futilely delaying the inevitable.

He might not be a college graduate, he thought ruefully, but he was certainly bright enough to take a hint and read the signs—especially if Claire was beating him over the head with one of them.

His marriage was over.

The sooner he came to terms with that, the sooner he would...

Would what?

Heal? he asked himself, mocking the very thought.

Heal for what reason? So that he could someday fall

for someone else and get to go through this all over again? So he could set himself up for another fall? No, living through this brutal experience once was more than enough for him.

Even the most thickheaded of creatures eventually learned their lesson, and it was time for him to learn his. In this case, his lesson was that he was the kind of man who was destined to be abandoned time and again. His father hadn't wanted to stick around. Who knew? Maybe his mother wouldn't have, either, if it wasn't for the fact that she also had two younger sons besides him at home.

Levi pressed his lips together. That wasn't fair, and he knew it. He was just allowing the situation to get the better of him.

He had tried, really honestly *tried*, to be the best husband and father he could be. But without an example to follow, he admittedly was just blindly moving through his days, doing what he *thought* was the right thing without really knowing if he was succeeding.

Levi laughed shortly at himself.

Obviously, he *hadn't* succeeded because if he had, he would have been home in his apartment with Claire and the baby, and all this would have been moot.

And it wasn't.

Levi blinked to clear his vision and focus. He'd been so preoccupied with this new course of action he was plotting for himself that he hadn't realized that he'd driven the entire way back.

The route had gotten to be so automatic for him that

he'd just driven without watching, and he was now parked behind the boarding house.

For a second he just remained where he was, not wanting to move, not wanting to begin implementing what was to be the last leg of his failed union with Claire. And then he shrugged. He supposed he might as well get this over with.

He had to view this the way he viewed removing a Band-Aid from a wound. He had to strike fast and keep it neat. That would help keep the pain at a minimum.

Who the hell was he kidding? The pain wasn't going to be kept at a minimum. The pain was going to be devastating. But it still had to happen.

Opening the front door, Levi glanced in the direction of the dining room and then the kitchen. The pull he experienced to just walk to either one of the rooms in hopes of seeing Claire was strong, but he forced himself to ignore it.

Why prolong his agony? No matter what, it was going to end the same way. He had to do what he had to do and do it like a man, not like a whimpering child.

So instead of going to either room with the hopes of catching a glimpse of Claire, he went straight to the front stairs and headed up to the second floor and his room.

He had things to pack.

Claire frowned as she craned her neck and looked out of the kitchen and down the hall. She could have sworn she'd heard the front door open and then close again. At this hour, that had to be Levi. This was about the time that he'd been coming in the past few weeks.

Then again, maybe he'd stayed at the store longer, she thought. Doing some of that overtime he always talked about.

But would he do that, considering how things were between them right now? she asked herself, playing her own devil's advocate. No, she was fairly sure that he wouldn't.

That meant that perhaps he'd already come home and had just gone up to his room. He could very well be up there at this moment.

Gina looked in her direction and obviously noticed her preoccupation. "Something wrong?" Gina asked.

Claire had noticed that as a rule, Gina did not pry. That the older woman was even asking this question meant that she wasn't masking her feelings very well.

Even so, her first reaction was denial. "No, nothing's wrong." And then Claire paused, rethinking her words. "Well, maybe," she admitted, vacillating.

And then she made up her mind. What was she doing, standing here, talking to Gina, when she could be upstairs, saving her marriage? It was no contest.

"I'll be right back," she told Gina, stripping the apron off and leaving it slung over the back of one of the chairs.

Gina nodded, as if she understood the chaotic thoughts that were bouncing off one another in her head.

"Take your time," Gina advised. "We're almost finished here anyway."

Claire fervently hoped that the statement couldn't also be applied to her own situation with Levi.

Hurrying out of the kitchen, Claire passed her grandfather holding her daughter in his arms just outside the door.

"Look who's here, Bekka. Your mama's rushing to see you—"

"Grandpa, I need a few more minutes," she began, not really sure how to frame the problem she was currently facing.

Fortunately, in her grandfather's eyes, she could do no wrong, and he was more than willing to do anything she wanted him to.

"No problem, Claire-bear. That just means more time for me to spend with the princess here." He cuddled his cheek against the baby's. "Isn't that right, princess?"

Bekka made some sort of a cooing noise, as if she understood the question that had been put to her and was agreeing with her great-grandfather.

Claire breathed a sigh of relief. She needed a few minutes alone with Levi if she was going to convince him that she meant what she was saying.

Patting Gene's arm just before she flew up the stairs, she said, "Thank you, Grandpa. You're the best!"

"Tell your grandmother that," he told her, calling up the stairs after her disappearing form.

"I will," she called back. "I promise."

Mentally, she was already far away from the conversation with her grandfather.

Never superstitious, Claire still crossed her fingers.

Just let this go well, please, she prayed.

Claire stopped just a few steps short of her husband's door. Taking a deep breath, she tried the doorknob.

Expecting to find it open, she turned the knob only to discover that it didn't give. Levi had locked his door. Since when?

A chill zipped up and down her spine, making all of her feel cold.

This was a bad sign, she thought, looking at the door.

Releasing the doorknob, Claire began to turn away. And then, out of nowhere, she heard her grandmother's voice in her head. It was mocking her.

Giving up already? You're no granddaughter of mine if you do.

"Oh, yes, I am," Claire caught herself saying out loud. She had to watch that, she silently upbraided herself. She didn't want anyone thinking she was talking to herself.

The next moment she knocked on Levi's door. "Levi? Are you in there?" She knocked again, more loudly this time. "Levi?"

There was still no answer.

Her pulse quickened. She was making a fool of herself, Claire thought. She was standing out here, knocking on his door, and he probably wasn't in.

And, if he *was* in, then that was even worse because it meant that he was ignoring her.

Well, what did you expect? That he was just going to be standing in the shadows, pining away for you until you gave him the time of day? Give it up.

Her heart ached as she turned away from the door. Claire had taken a total of three steps toward the stairs when she heard the door behind her opening.

Hope suddenly renewed and bursting out inside her, she swung around to see if it was Levi, or if someone else had opened their door to see what all the commotion was about.

It wasn't *someone else*, it was Levi.

A very solemn-looking Levi with flat, unreadable eyes.

This isn't good, a little voice in her head whispered.

All that meant was that she had to make this good, that same voice told her.

The problem was, she wasn't sure if she could anymore.

"Is something wrong with Bekka?" Levi asked, concerned. He couldn't think of any other reason why Claire would come to his door, looking for him.

Levi had given her an excuse to use, and she almost ran with it. But then she stopped herself. The truth. She needed to stick with the truth. That was the only way this was going to work between them.

Levi respected the truth. What he didn't respect, she recalled, were women who played silly games. That was one of the first things he had ever said to her, telling her that he was grateful that she didn't believe in playing games.

"Nothing's wrong with Bekka," she told Levi quietly. And then she took a deep breath and said, almost all in one breath, "There's something wrong with me."

The concern on his face instantly multiplied a dozenfold. Taking her hand in his, Levi asked her, "Are you sick?"

Granted, she felt a little light-headed, but that could have been due to any one of a number of reasons. And right now it would be squandering the moment if she talked about anything else but what she needed to get off her chest.

"May I come in?"

"Sure." Levi stepped back and opened his door. "Sit," he instructed, gesturing toward the bed. One question came swiftly on the heels of another. "Do you want a glass of water? Do you want me to call your grandmother—?"

"No. And no," Claire told him with finality. "I don't need water or my grandmother. What I need is you," she told him slowly, as if she was testing out each word on the tip of her tongue before she said it out loud.

Since he had come to the boarding house and registered for a room just to be near Claire and the baby, he'd allowed his spirits to rise up more than a dozen times, only to have them come crashing down time and again. This time, he kept a tight rein on them.

"I don't understand."

She opened her mouth to explain, then stopped. For the first time Claire looked around the room he'd been living in these past few weeks.

Claire noted that he had both his suitcases on the bed, opened. They were both more than half-filled. Her uneasiness increased.

"Going on a trip?" she asked, doing her best to make her voice sound innocent.

His eyes met hers and held them for a long moment. "Going back," he corrected. "To the apartment."

"You're leaving?" Claire asked numbly, even as something in her head was screaming not to allow that to happen.

"Yeah," he confirmed, shutting the door behind her. "I guess the plus side of that will be that I won't be bothering you anymore."

"What if…" Her voice suddenly evaporated, and she had to concentrate on finding it again. Clearing her throat, Claire tried once more. "What if I said I wanted you to bother me?"

Levi stared at her, wondering what was going on and why she'd say something like that when she couldn't possibly mean it.

"I'd say that nothing would make me happier—but we both know that you're just yanking my chain. I'm not going to hang around here and hope that I wear you down. I don't want you by default. I want you because you want to be with me. Because you love me at least half as much as I love you.

"But I know that I can't make you love me," he continued, his spirit flagging, "and—"

"What about the other night?" she wanted to know, pulling out all the stops. "We made love, and that was pretty special."

"It was more than that."

Pretty special seemed like such a tiny, meaningless

phrase to apply to what had transpired between them. "But it's still not enough," Levi told her. "I want more than just chemistry, Claire. More than just Fourth of July rockets exploding between us. I want—I *need*— the whole package."

He looked at her for a very long moment, framing the last of his summation. "Most of all, I don't want to constantly have to worry that you're going to leave me. That it's just a matter of time before I come home one night to find that you've packed up and left with the baby. Part of me says I should be happy with what I can get, but I can't live that way anymore, Claire. It's just not fair to—"

"You're right," Claire agreed wholeheartedly, jumping the gun and filling in his last word. "It's not fair to you."

That wasn't what he meant. He felt that the way it stood, it was an unfair situation for the both of them, not just him.

"I didn't say that—"

"Well, you should have," she told Levi, cutting him off. And then she had an idea. "Can I use your bathroom for a second?"

The request seemed to come completely out of nowhere and threw him for a second.

But then Levi shrugged and indicated the closed door to the tiny powder room. "Sure. Go ahead. It's right through there. I'll just get back to my packing," he told her, turning away.

She'd almost left then. Seeing the suitcases and

watching him get back to packing, her courage plummeted strongly.

But then she squared her shoulders and silently told herself, *It's now or never. Grandmother had it right. If something was worth having, it was worth fighting for.*

She closed the powder room door behind her.

Chapter Fifteen

Ordinarily, this would be exactly the time when she would touch up her makeup, make sure that she was, visually, the very best version of herself that she could possibly be. That would involve making sure that her dress—or a skimpy top and abbreviated shorts— showed her off to her best advantage.

She'd also make sure that her hair was combed into a lustrous sheen if she was wearing it down, and if it happened to be up, she would strategically dispense colored-crystal clips discreetly throughout.

That was her total package, and it left no man unaffected.

But tonight, here in Levi's tiny powder room, there were no crystal hairclips, no extra, secret little rituals that helped her create this complete picture of perfection she was usually so desperate to project. Beneath it all, she was certain that she was downright plain.

Claire stared at herself in the framed mirror that took the place of the outside of a medicine cabinet. Then she turned on the faucet and scrubbed her face clean, dried off with a towel and looked back into the mirror.

Well, there she was, Claire thought, just as God had created her. Maybe not entirely a plain Jane, but certainly not a "Jane" who was guaranteed to take a man's breath away.

"Okay," she told the reflection in the mirror. "Time to face the music and show the man what he really wound up getting when he said *I do*."

"Claire?" Levi's voice came through the bathroom door, calling out to her.

Claire froze.

Could he possibly have caught a glimpse of her through a crack in the door?

Turning, she looked at the door that separated them. There was no crack evident. Claire told herself to calm down.

"Yes?" she asked a little hesitantly.

"Who are you talking to?" Levi wanted to know.

"Just myself," she answered. Then so he wouldn't think she was crazy, she added as an explanation, "Working up my courage."

The reply puzzled him more than it answered anything. "Courage for what?"

Putting her hand on the doorknob, Claire slowly turned it. The resulting sound of the tongue leaving the groove, allowing her to open the door, seemed to echo extra loudly in her head, like a final warning sound. She knew that once she stepped out of the powder room and into his bedroom, there would be no turning back.

Her breath seemed to shorten, and the whole procedure felt as if it was taking place in slow motion.

"For this," she told him in a small, hollow voice. Her mouth felt as dry as a desert as she came out and stood before him.

Levi looked at her. He shook his head, not in disapproval but in complete confusion.

"This?" he repeated, completely mystified. "What are you talking about, Claire?"

She couldn't believe that he didn't see it. He had to be pulling her leg. Either that, or the man was so used to her, he wasn't "seeing" her the way she really was, but the way he perceived her in his mind.

"This," she repeated more insistently. She swept her hand up and down in the vicinity of her face. By the look on Levi's face, he still wasn't seeing it. How could he not? "Don't tell me you don't see it," she said incredulously.

He still had no idea what she was talking about. "What I'm seeing is my wife."

"And—?" she asked, trying to lead him to what she believed was the most important part of this soul-searching moment.

"And she looks nice," Levi concluded. But by the exasperated look on Claire's face, that wasn't what she wanted to hear. "Okay, no more games, Claire. What is it you want me to say?"

She threw up her hands, giving up. "I'm not wearing any makeup, Levi. *None,*" she cried. Just how blind *was* he?

He nodded his head, although his expression didn't change. He didn't appear to be a man who had suddenly experienced enlightenment. "I can see that. And I like it better."

That was *not* what she was expecting. "What?"

"I like it better," he repeated. "You look, I don't know, cleaner, fresher." And then he smiled as he said, "Prettier. All that makeup, it always made me feel like I was supposed to be taking you out to some expensive restaurant. It also made me feel that you were just killing time with me until someone better came along, someone who could give you a fancy lifestyle that I couldn't afford—yet," he added, because he fully intended to, someday.

She was having trouble coming to terms with his reaction to her soul-baring experiment. Cocking her head, she tried to read between the lines. Tried to discover if this man was on the level.

"You're actually telling me that you like me *better* this way?"

He didn't want to hurt her feelings or insult her, but the truth was the truth.

"I suppose I am. You look more genuine," he confessed. Since his answer was obviously not making her very happy, he was quick to add, "Not that you're not beautiful with all the stuff on your face, but you just look more…real."

They'd been married nearly two years. Before that, they had been together for two years. And she had never let him see her without her makeup in all that time. "If you felt that way, why didn't you say anything sooner?" she wanted to know.

"Tell you I thought you had on too much makeup?" Levi questioned. "Claire, I might not be the sharpest knife in the drawer, but I'm not a complete idiot, and I don't harbor a death wish. I know better than to tell a beautiful woman she's being heavy-handed with her makeup. Besides, it seemed to make you happy, and I wasn't going to criticize something that made you feel good about yourself."

Claire felt as if she was shell-shocked. She wanted to be sure she absorbed this properly. "So you really, truly *like* me this way?"

"*Like* is a very weak word," Levi pointed out. "I *love* you this way."

Her eyes searched his face to make sure that she'd heard him correctly. And then they strayed to his bed and the opened luggage on it.

"If that's the case, why are the suitcases still out?" she asked.

Since she had let down her hair, so to speak, he felt it was safe to be honest with her the way she was asking him to be. "Because I can't live with the uncertainty anymore."

It was her turn to look confused. Older and more

sophisticated than she was, he had always struck her as the pillar of confidence. This was all news to her. "Uncertainty?"

Levi blew out a breath. This was harder than he imagined. "I was sure that you were going to leave me again the very next time we have an argument."

"You're right," she answered simply.

"Then you *were* going to leave the very next time we had an argument?" Maybe he should be putting that in the present tense, he thought. The pain that caused him hurt his heart.

"No," she corrected, "you're right that you shouldn't have to live this way. Let's just call that our period of adjustment—we were ironing out the kinks of being two married people with a baby. A baby always adds a lot of extra stress until we both learn how to successfully juggle your job, our lives and the baby's needs. And while we're talking about our faults—" She paused for a second, biting her lower lip as she thought about what she was going to say and how to word it.

"I was wrong."

Levi had the distinct feeling that they were waltzing around not one issue but a number of them. "Wrong about what?"

Since she was apologizing, she might as well give it to him with all the trimmings. There was nothing to be gained by being evasive.

"Wrong about getting so upset because you went to play poker and hang out with some of the local guys.

Adults need 'playtime,' too," she told Levi encouragingly.

Levi's mouth dropped open as he stared at his wife. "You're serious?"

She nodded. "Completely. I guess…sometimes it takes me a while to come to my senses. I just felt abandoned every morning when you went off to work, leaving me with the dirty dishes, a crying baby and my ever-depleting feelings of self-worth."

Stunned, he rounded the side of the bed and came closer to Claire, his suitcases and the clothes he was putting into them temporarily forgotten about. They could always be packed later.

She'd caught his attention with an almost throwaway line. The line made absolutely no sense to him. "Why would your feelings of self-worth be depleted?"

There were a lot of answers to that. She gave him the simplest one. "I couldn't even calm down a baby. My grandfather's better at it than I am."

There were reasons for that. "Number one, your grandfather helped raise four boys, and he tells me that the more experience you have with kids, the easier it is to raise them. You were learning how to deal with all that at your own pace," he told her encouragingly. "And I guess I wasn't all that supportive."

He expected her to agree. When she didn't, he began to feel that maybe there was hope for them after all.

"You were trying to make sure that you were earning enough money so that Bekka never needed anything. It couldn't have been easy, pushing yourself like that. Especially when all you had to come home to was a complaining wife."

Feeling a certain lightness had him playfully teasing her. "Hey, don't be so hard on my wife. She had her reasons." He paused, looking at her closely. "So I guess maybe we do have a chance of making this work?" He ended with a question, but there was definitely a hopeful note in his voice.

Her smile was from ear to ear. "I sure hope so. Oh, Levi, I am *so* ready to go home."

He took her into his arms, wrapping them around her as he brought her close to him. "I think we already are home."

She looked at him, puzzled. "Here?" she questioned, looking around the tiny room.

"I'm going to talk to your grandparents, see if maybe we could get one of the larger rooms for the three of us and stay on for a while." He told her his news, news that had all but seemed irrelevant this morning, but now it could very well be the key to straightening out their lives. "The furniture chain is opening up a new branch in Kalispell, which is a lot closer for me so I won't be gone as long as I used to be each day."

She nodded, taking it in. It all sounded like maybe their lives were finally coming together. "And I could go on working here at the boarding house. Grandmother wants me to be the assistant cook. I really didn't think I could manage the job, but it seems to be coming together," she told him proudly. "Cooking is working out pretty well for me. Even my grandmother can't find anything to complain about with my cooking. Or, if Grandmother decides to go back to cooking here herself—she mentioned that she misses doing it, and Gina and her husband are considering moving to Bozeman, to be closer to their kids, so who knows what might happen. And, if Grandmother does go back to cooking here, I could get a part-time job at the day care."

He laughed, enjoying his wife's enthusiasm. "Hey, you can do anything you set your mind to."

She was fixated on her part in this new plan. "I'm thinking if I had that part-time job, then maybe you wouldn't have to work as many hours as you do—and we could spend more time together as a family."

He smiled into her eyes. "Sounds good to me. *Really* good," he told her, lightly kissing her temple, creating a delicious warmth within her. "Let's make a deal," he told her.

"A deal?" She wasn't sure where he was going with this. She wasn't leery—she loved him—but she tried to brace herself.

He nodded. "Whatever we do from here on in, we're going to make our decisions together. As a family. None of this stoically taking on more than we should and then expecting that the other person's going to be all right with it without at least hearing the argument for it. Does that sound like something you can live with?" he asked her.

"As long as I can live with you, that's all I care about." She felt as if a huge, huge boulder had been lifted from

her heart. "And you're sure that you're okay with looking at me like this?" she had to ask one last time.

"Perfectly okay," he told her. And then he dead-
panned, "I figure if I haven't been turned to stone yet,
the odds are pretty good in my favor."

Claire doubled up her fist and punched him in the
arm. He laughed, pretending to wince.

"There's my Claire," he announced, delighted. "You
haven't done that in a long time."

"I could pummel you to the ground and make up for
lost time," she offered.

"I think I'll take a pass on that for now. Besides, if
you pummel me to the ground, how am I going to be
able to do this?" he asked, kissing first one cheek and
then the other.

"Good point," she murmured, feeling the kernel of
excitement pop within her inner core and flowering into
all the surrounding regions. "Wouldn't want to stifle
your creative instincts."

"Speaking of creative instincts, how much longer do
you think we can count on your grandfather entertaining Bekka and keeping her with him?"

"Indefinitely," she answered. "He usually hangs on
to Bekka until I come to his room to collect her."

Levi's expression brightened. "So if we don't show
up for a couple of hours to claim her—"

"Grandpa will be, as they like to say, 'in hog heaven.'"

Claire wasn't sure just what was going on. "Why are
you asking about Bekka?"

He spared her a long, penetrating look. "Just wanted to be sure that she's not going to suddenly show up at the wrong time."

Claire laughed as she suddenly had a vision of their eight-month-old standing outside their door, plotting to get even for being left with a sitter.

"Not on her own, she wouldn't. She's only a little older than eight months, remember? Babies don't walk at eight months."

"But they do see."

"Yesss." She stretched out the word, waiting to see where he was going with this.

"I think her education should begin a little later, not now."

"You're planning to do something educational with me?" she asked innocently, humor dancing in her eyes.

"Not exactly educational," he allowed. "I think I'd place this in the realm of entertainment instead. Entertainment and pleasure." He smiled. "Think I could interest you in, oh, perhaps getting a sample?"

"I think you could interest me in getting a complete course in the subject."

"I was hoping you'd say that." Just before he kissed her, he framed her face with his hand. "God, but I have missed you."

"I'm right here, Levi. And I'm not going anywhere."

"Amen to that," he murmured just before he lowered his mouth to hers.

"I love you, Claire," he said against her mouth before there wasn't room for any more talk.

At the last possible second, she said, "I love you, too," sending the rest of their marriage off to a wonderfully promising start.

Epilogue

Her eyes still closed, Claire stretched beneath the sheet. Ever so slowly, she shed the confining restraints of sleep from her body.

It took her brain a beat to catch up.

When it did, the fact that her arm didn't come in contact with another body registered. The place beside her in bed was empty.

Her eyes flew open as the significance of that fact sank in.

Levi wasn't next to her.

After making love in his room last night, they had both gotten dressed and gone down together to her grandfather to retrieve Bekka. The old man offered to keep the little girl with him overnight, but they had politely refused. Neither she nor Levi wanted to be that obvious about their reconciliation—yet.

As if she somehow sensed that her parents needed more time together, the baby had fallen right to sleep the moment they laid her down and for once, she didn't wake up crying two or three times during the course of the night. Instead, she'd slept straight through, leaving Levi and her to reexplore the joys of sleeping in the same bed all over again.

Claire couldn't remember when she'd felt as happy as she had when she'd fallen asleep last night.

But this morning was a different story.

She woke up to an empty bed—and an empty crib, she suddenly realized. It was not only Levi who was missing, but it was the baby, too.

Bekka was nowhere to be seen.

Had the baby woken up sick? Had Levi taken her downstairs to her grandmother for help? Or maybe he'd driven Bekka over to the hospital.

Without telling her?

Why wouldn't he wake her up and tell her he was taking the baby to the hospital?

A panic began to set in, stealing her very breath away.

Throwing off the sheet, Claire was about to pull on the first clothes she found when she heard the door opening.

Levi walked in carrying Bekka in one arm while holding a mostly empty baby bottle in the other.

"Oh, look, Bekka, Mommy's up—and she's naked."

Levi then quickly reversed his instructions. "Don't look, Bekka."

Flushing, although more from annoyance than embarrassment, Claire grabbed the robe that was on the floor at the foot of her bed. She assumed it must have slipped off during last night's activities.

"Where were you?" she wanted to know. "You had me really worried."

Levi placed the baby into her crib then joined Claire. He paused to brush his lips against hers.

"Nice to know you worry, but Bekka was fussing and I thought you deserved to sleep in a little bit, especially after that encore performance last night," he added with a wink.

"So you took her downstairs?" Claire asked, surprised.

"Had to eventually. That was where her formula was," Levi explained when she looked at him quizzically.

Claire decided that sounded as plausible as any other explanation. She turned her attention to the baby.

"She's probably soaking wet by now. I'd better change her—"

"Already done," Levi said, stopping her in her tracks.

Claire looked at him in amazement. "Boy, one day on the job and you've gotten better at it than me," she commented.

He was quick to negate her assessment. "That could never happen, not even if I was on the job a hundred years. All I want to do is help," he told her with sincerity.

"You help," Claire assured him. "Just by being here, you help a lot." Tightening the sash at her waist, she proceeded to make her bed. She was going to have to be in the kitchen soon, she thought as she worked her way around the perimeter of the bed.

When she got to Levi's side, she stopped dead. There was a lump under the sheet just beneath his pillow. When she started to smooth it out, she discovered that the lump wasn't caused by a crumpled sheet, it was caused by a black velvet box. She looked at it, and then at Levi. "What's this?"

"Best way to find out is to open it," he told her casually.

Her hands were steady, but she was trembling inside as she slowly drew back the top of the box. Inside the ring box was her wedding ring, gleaming the way it hadn't in two years.

"My ring," she cried. Raising her eyes to his, she asked, "It *is* my wedding ring, right?"

"It is your wedding ring," he confirmed.

"But I looked everywhere for it," she told him, remembering how bitterly unhappy she'd been to lose it. "How did you—?"

"When you threw it at me, it fell onto the floor in the hall, and of course I picked it up so it wouldn't get lost. I held on to it hoping you'd want it—and me—back someday." Taking the box from her, he took the ring out and held it up to her. "Claire Strickland, will you do me the very great honor of becoming my wife—again?"

"Yes!" She threw her arms around him, hugging him tightly. "Oh, yes!"

Levi tugged at her sash and then slipped his arms in beneath her robe.

Claire forgot all about getting ready for work.

They both did.

* * * * *

*Don't miss the next installment of the new
Harlequin Special Edition continuity*

MONTANA MAVERICKS:
WHAT HAPPENED AT THE WEDDING?

*Lani Dalton doesn't trust men—not even one who
carries a badge. Russ Campbell was burned by love
and would rather stay single forever than risk his
heart again. But when they team up to figure out who
spiked the wedding punch on July Fourth, a perfectly
imperfect match may occur!*

*Look for
AN OFFICER AND A MAVERICK
by Teresa Southwick*

*On sale September 2015, wherever Harlequin books
and ebooks are sold.*

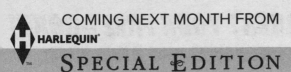
#2425 An Officer and a Maverick
Montana Mavericks: What Happened at the Wedding?
by Teresa Southwick

Lani Dalton needs to distract on-duty Officer Russ Campbell from her rowdy brother. Instead, they wind up locked in a cell together, where sparks ignite. Russ isn't eager to trust another woman after he had his heart stomped on once before...but the deputy might just lasso this darling Dalton for good!

#2426 The Bachelor Takes a Bride
Those Engaging Garretts!
by Brenda Harlen

Marco Palermo believes in love at first sight—now, if only he could get Jordyn Garrett to agree with him! A wager leads to a date and a sizzling kiss, but can Marco open Jordyn up to love and make her his forever?

#2427 Destined to Be a Dad
Welcome to Destiny
by Christyne Butler

Liam Murphy just discovered he's a daddy—fifteen years too late. The cowboy is taken with his daughter and her mother, Missy Dobbs. The beautiful Brit was the one who got away, but Liam knows Destiny, Wyoming, is where he and his girls are meant to be together.

#2428 A Sweetheart for the Single Dad
The Camdens of Colorado
by Victoria Pade

Tender-hearted Lindie Camden is making up for her family's misdeeds by helping out the Camdens' archrival, Sawyer Huffman, on a community project. Sawyer's good heart and even better looks soon have her dreaming of happily-ever-after with the sexy single dad...

#2429 Coming Home to a Cowboy
Family Renewal
by Sheri WhiteFeather

Horse trainer Kade Quinn heads to Montana after uncovering his long-lost son. But he remains wary of the child's mother, Bridget Wells. She once lit his body and heart on fire, and time hasn't dulled their passion for each other—and their family!

#2430 The Rancher's Surprise Son
Gold Buckle Cowboys
by Christine Wenger

Cowboy Cody Masters has only ever loved one woman—Laura, the beautiful daughter of his arrogant neighbor. So when he finds out that Laura had their child, he's shocked. Can Cody reclaim what's his and build the family he's always dreamed of with Laura and their son?

SPECIAL EXCERPT FROM

H HARLEQUIN®

SPECIAL EDITION

*Marco Palermo is convinced Jordyn Garrett is
The One for him. But it'll be a challenge to convince
the beautiful brunette to open her heart to him—and
the happily-ever-after only he can give her!*

*Read on for a sneak preview of
THE BACHELOR TAKES A BRIDE, the latest book in*
Brenda Harlen's popular miniseries,
*THOSE ENGAGING GARRETTS!:
THE CAROLINA COUSINS.*

He settled his hands lightly on her hips, holding her close but not too tight. He wanted her to know that this was her choice while leaving her in no doubt about what he wanted. She pressed closer to him, and the sensation of her soft curves against his body made him ache.

He parted her lips with his tongue and she opened willingly. She tasted warm and sweet—with a hint of vanilla from the coffee she'd drank—and the exquisite flavor of her spread through his blood, through his body, like an addictive drug.

He felt something bump against his shin. Once. Twice.

The cat, he realized, in the same moment he decided he didn't dare ignore its warning.

Not that he was afraid of Gryffindor, but he was afraid of scaring off Jordyn. Beneath her passionate response, he sensed a lingering wariness and uncertainty.

Slowly, reluctantly, he eased his lips from hers.

She drew in an unsteady breath, confusion swirling in her deep green eyes when she looked at him. "What... what just happened here?"

"I think we just confirmed that there's some serious chemistry between us."

She shook her head. "I'm not going to go out with you, Marco."

There was a note of something—almost like panic—in her voice that urged him to proceed cautiously. "I don't mind staying in," he said lightly.

She choked on a laugh. "I'm not going to have sex with you, either."

"Not tonight," he agreed. "I'm not *that* easy."

This time, she didn't quite manage to hold back the laugh, though sadness lingered in her eyes.

"You have a great laugh," he told her.

Her gaze dropped and her smile faded. "I haven't had much to laugh about in a while."

"Are you ever going to tell me about it?"

He braced himself for one of her flippant replies, a deliberate brush-off, and was surprised by her response.

"Maybe," she finally said. "But not tonight."

It was an acknowledgment that she would see him again, and that was enough for now.

Don't miss
THE BACHELOR TAKES A BRIDE
by Brenda Harlen,
available September 2015 wherever
Harlequin® Special Edition books and ebooks are sold.

www.Harlequin.com

Love the Harlequin book you just read?

Your opinion matters.

Review this book on your favorite book site, review site, blog or your own social media properties and share your opinion with other readers!

Be sure to connect with us at:
Harlequin.com/Newsletters
Facebook.com/HarlequinBooks
Twitter.com/HarlequinBooks

HARLEQUIN®

A *Romance* FOR EVERY MOOD™

Stay up-to-date on all your
romance-reading news with the
Harlequin Shopping Guide,
featuring bestselling authors, exciting new
miniseries, books to watch and more!

The newest issue will be delivered right to you
with our compliments! There are 4 each year.

Signing up is easy.

EMAIL

ShoppingGuide@Harlequin.ca

WRITE TO US

HARLEQUIN BOOKS
Attention: Customer Service Department
P.O. Box 9057, Buffalo, NY 14269-9057

OR PHONE

1-800-873-8635 in the United States
1-888-343-9777 in Canada

Please allow 4-6 weeks for delivery of the first issue by mail.

THE WORLD IS BETTER WITH

Romance

Harlequin has everything from contemporary, passionate and heartwarming to suspenseful and inspirational stories.

Whatever your mood, we have a romance just for you!